Bigfoot and Nessie
The Art of Getting Noticed

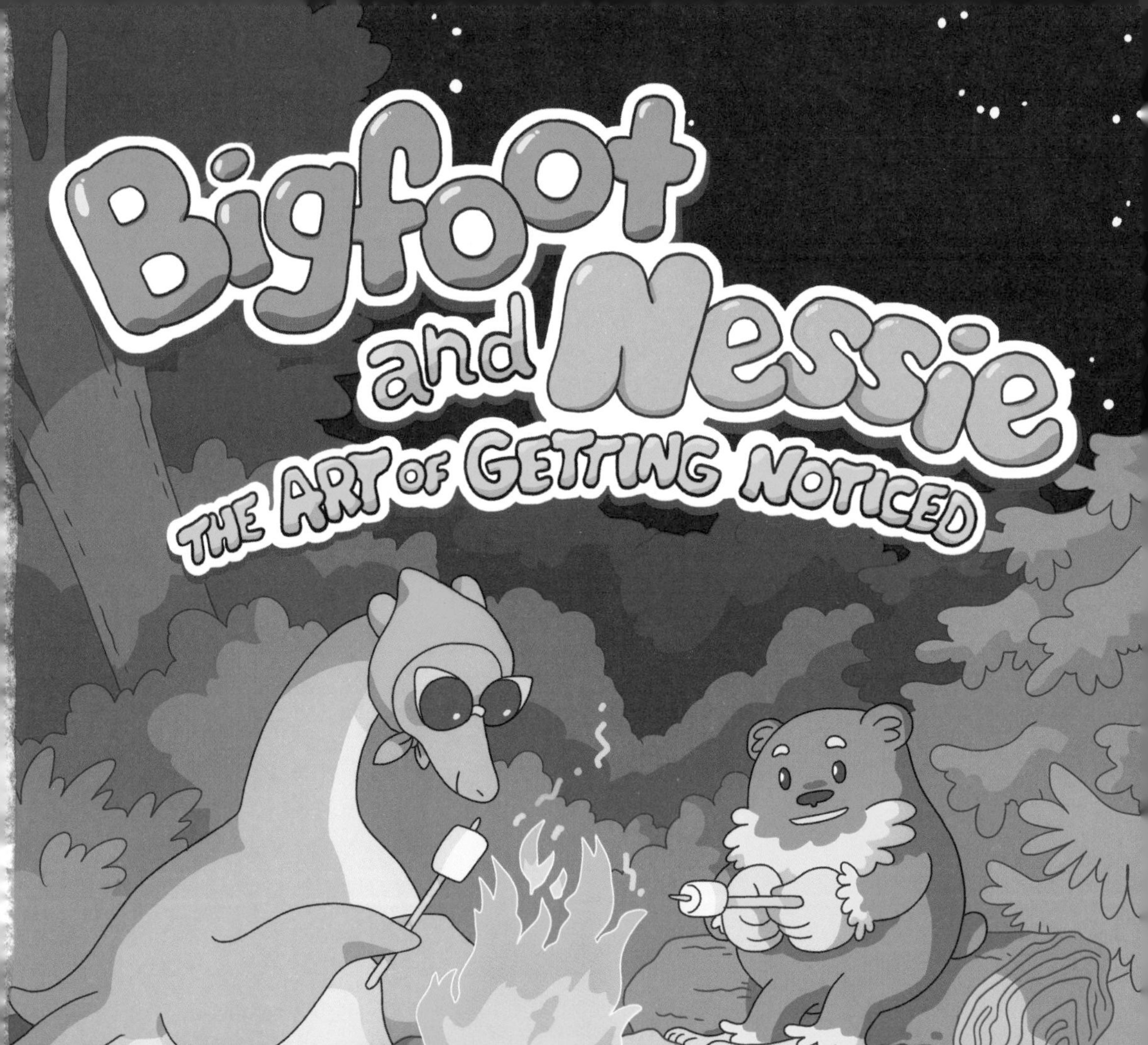

by Chelsea M. Campbell
and Laura Knetzger

Penguin Workshop

For Teisel, who loved
trying new things—CMC

For C—LK

PENGUIN WORKSHOP
An imprint of Penguin Random House LLC, New York

First published in the United States of America by Penguin Workshop,
an imprint of Penguin Random House LLC, New York, 2023

Visit us online at penguinrandomhouse.com.

Library of Congress Cataloging-in-Publication Data is available.

Manufactured in China

ISBN 9780593385722   10 9 8 7 6 5 4 3 2 1 WKT

Design by Jay Emmanuel
Lettering by Tess Stone

The publisher does not have any control over and does not assume any responsibility for author or third-party websites or their content.

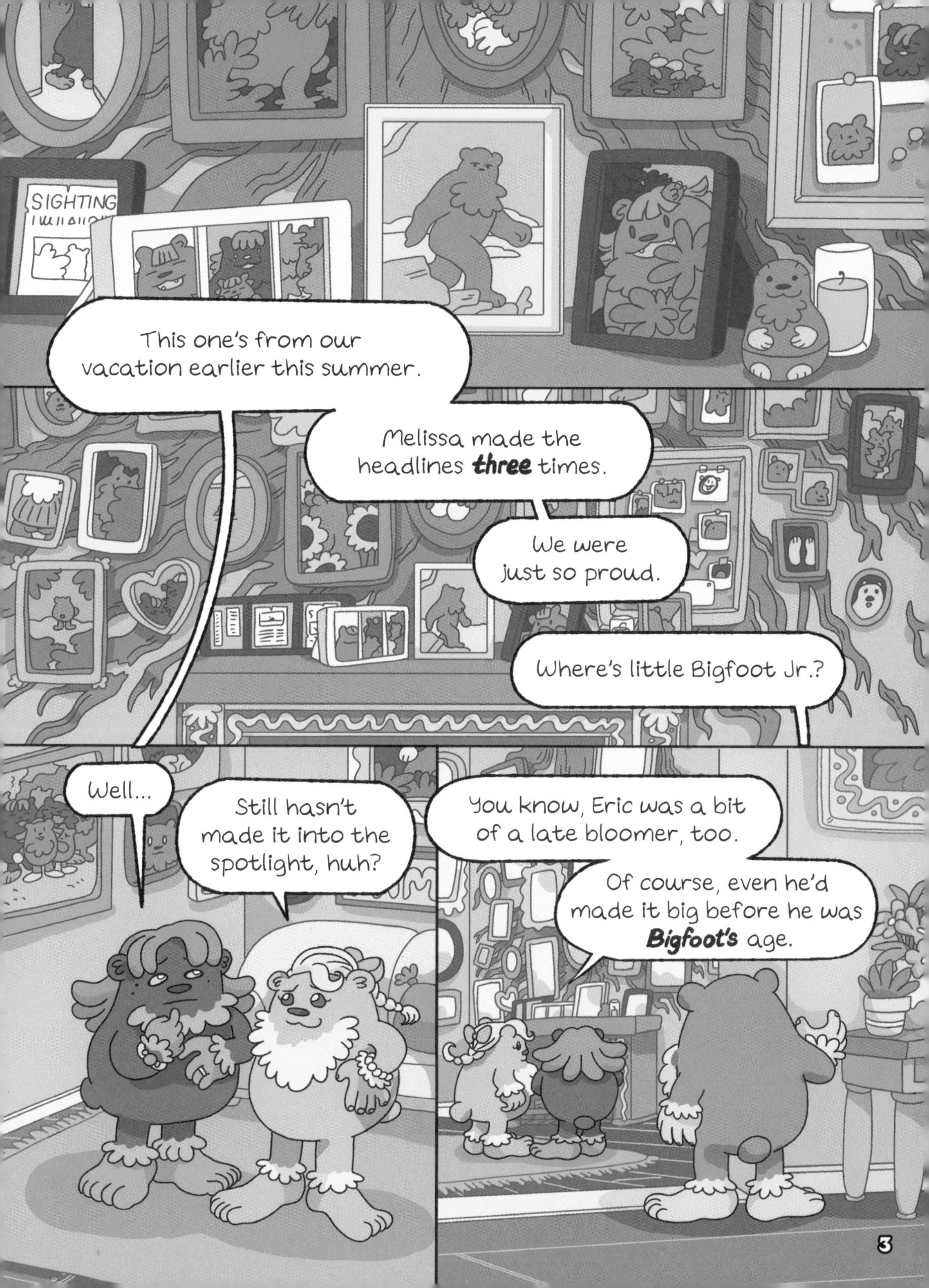
SIGHTING
This one's from our vacation earlier this summer.
Melissa made the headlines **three** times.
We were just so proud.
Where's little Bigfoot Jr.?
Well...
Still hasn't made it into the spotlight, huh?
You know, Eric was a bit of a late bloomer, too.
Of course, even he'd made it big before he was **Bigfoot's** age.

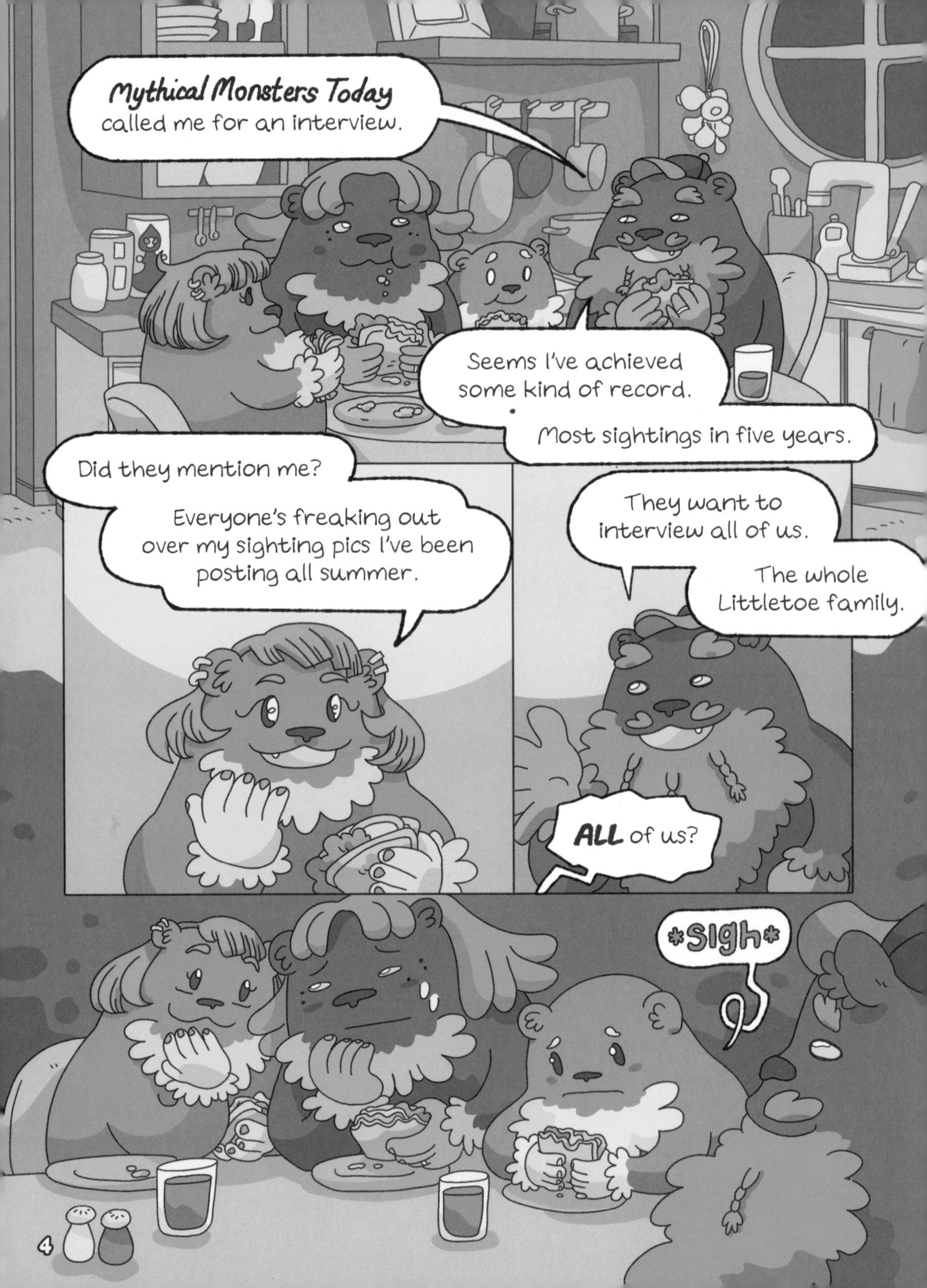
Mythical Monsters Today
called me for an interview.
Seems I've achieved some kind of record.
Most sightings in five years.
Did they mention me?
Everyone's freaking out over my sighting pics I've been posting all summer.
They want to interview all of us.
The whole Littletoe family.
ALL of us?
Sigh

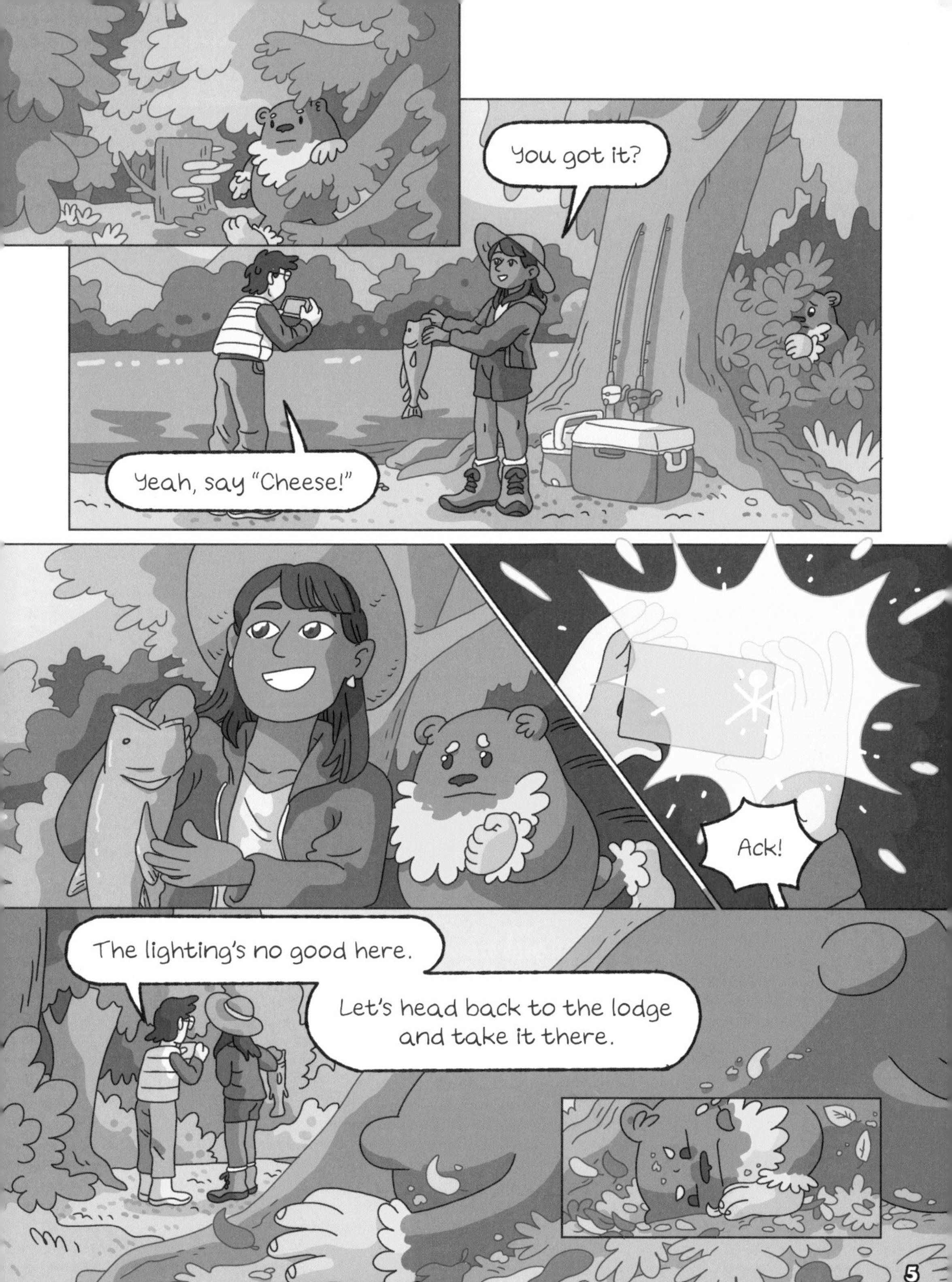

You got it?
Yeah, say "Cheese!"
Ack!
The lighting's no good here.
Let's head back to the lodge and take it there.

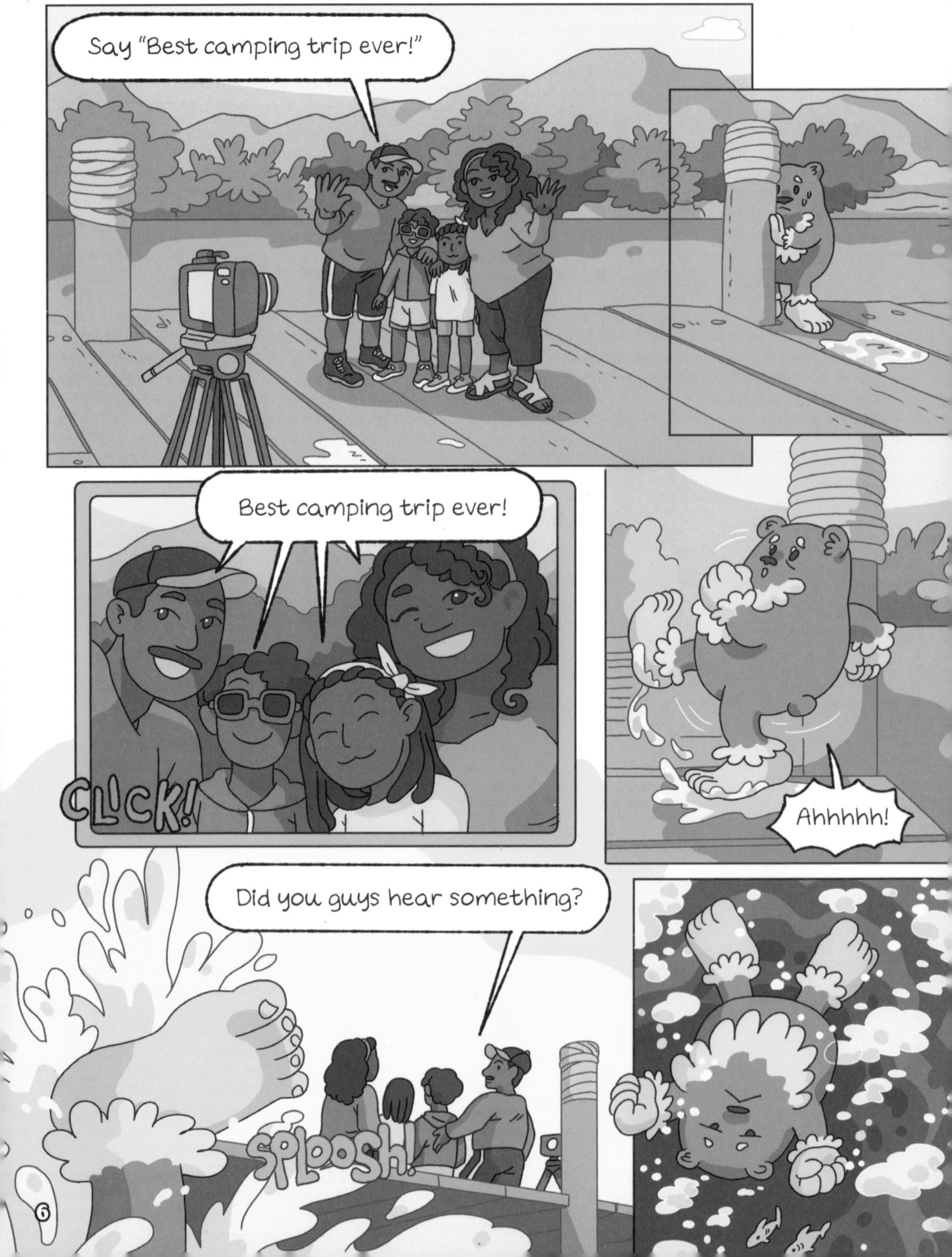

Say "Best camping trip ever!"
Best camping trip ever!
CLICK!
Ahhhhh!
Did you guys hear something?
SPLOOSH!

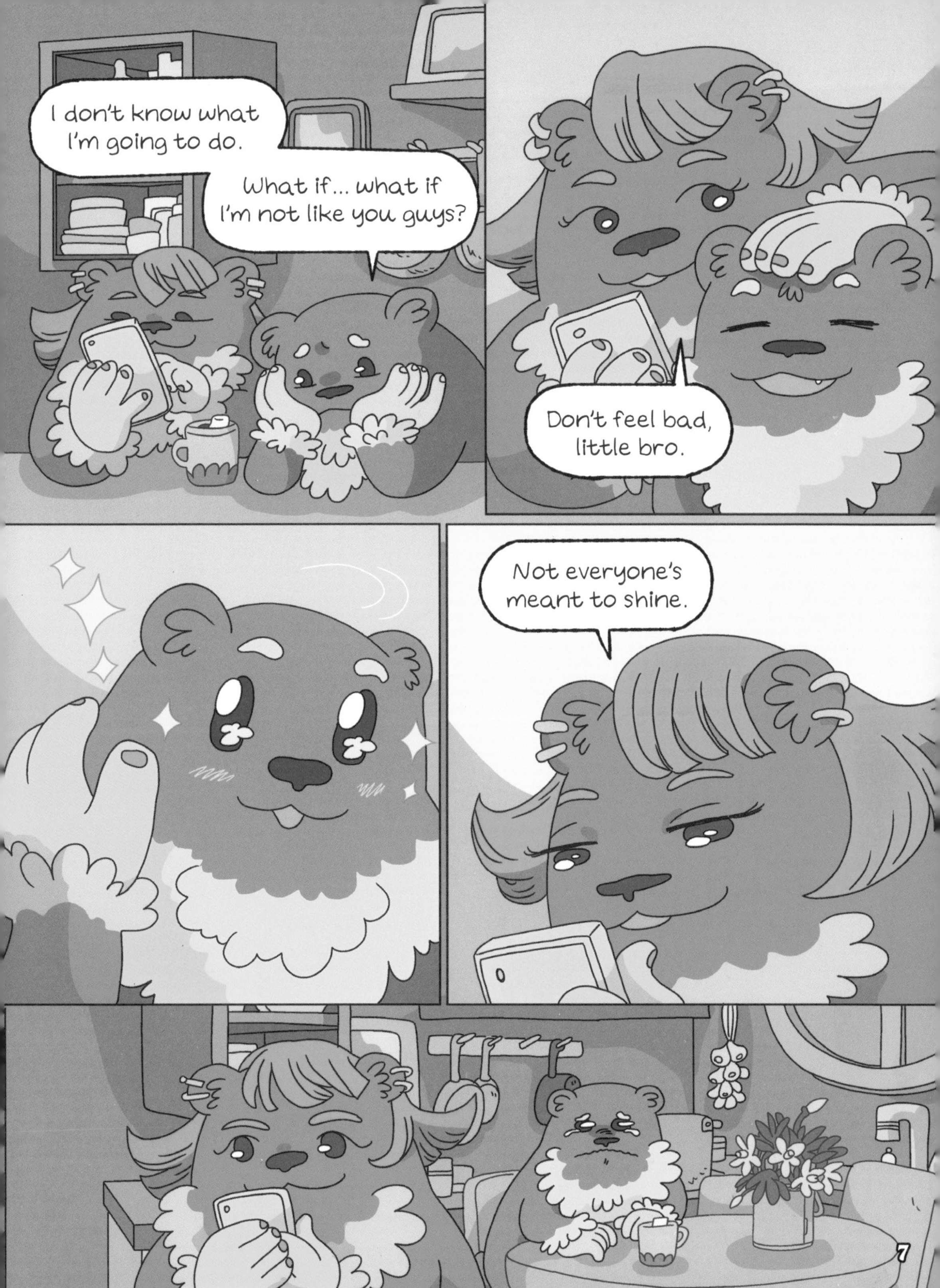

I don't know what I'm going to do.
What if... what if I'm not like you guys?
Don't feel bad, little bro.
Not everyone's meant to shine.

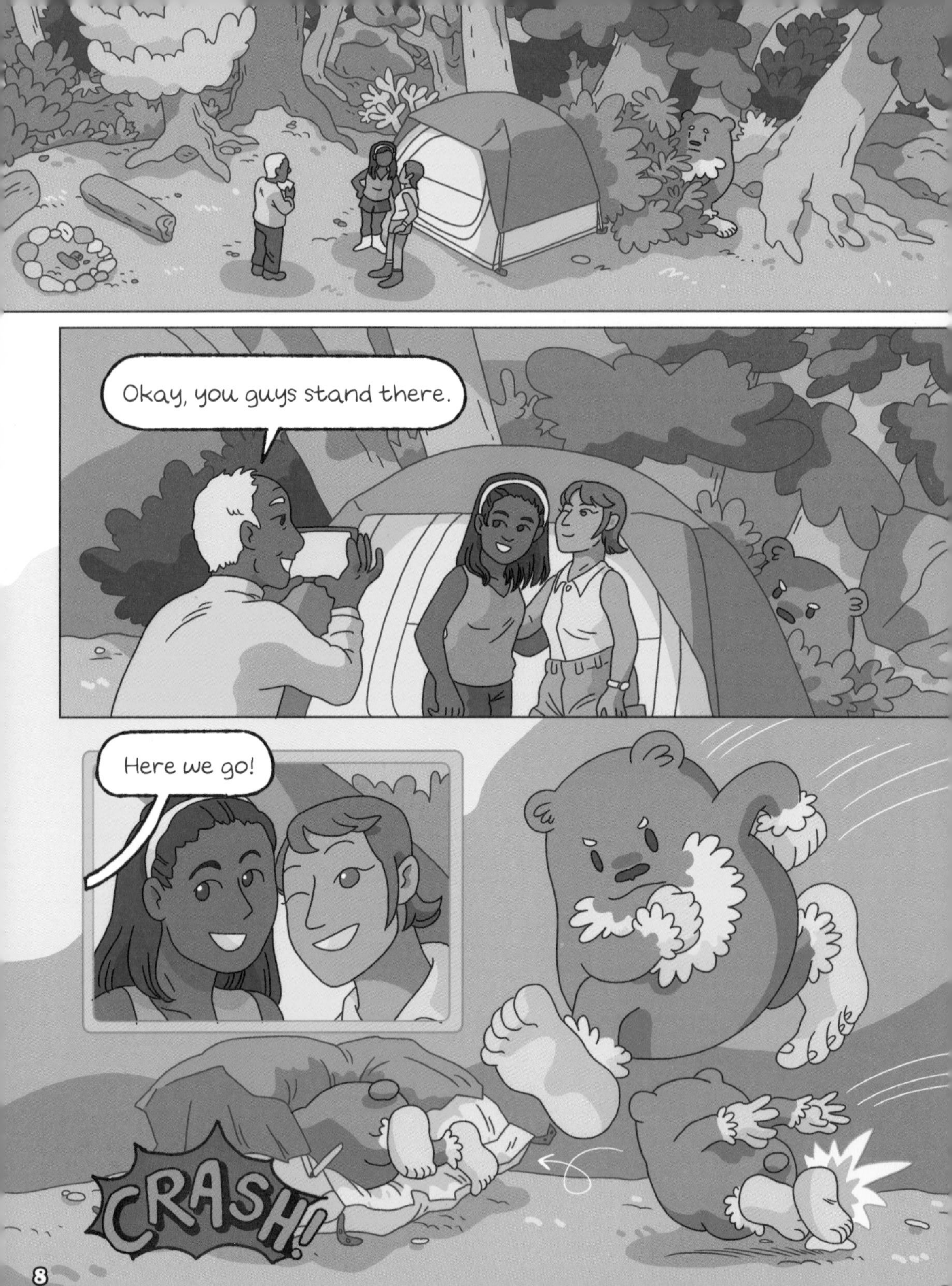
Okay, you guys stand there.
Here we go!
CRASH!

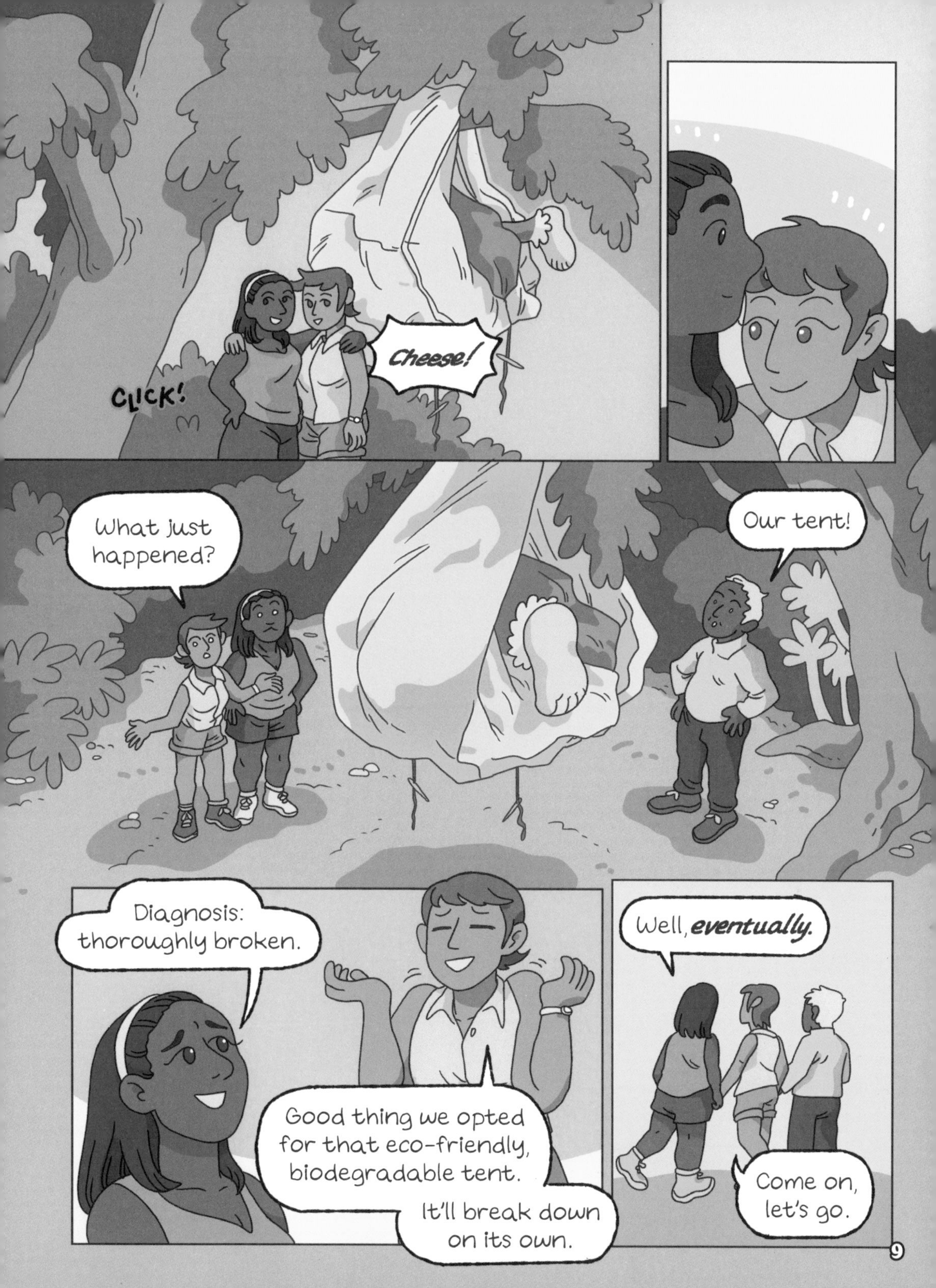
CLICK!
Cheese!
What just happened?
Our tent!
Diagnosis: thoroughly broken.
Good thing we opted for that eco-friendly, biodegradable tent.
It'll break down on its own.
Well, ***eventually.***
Come on, let's go.

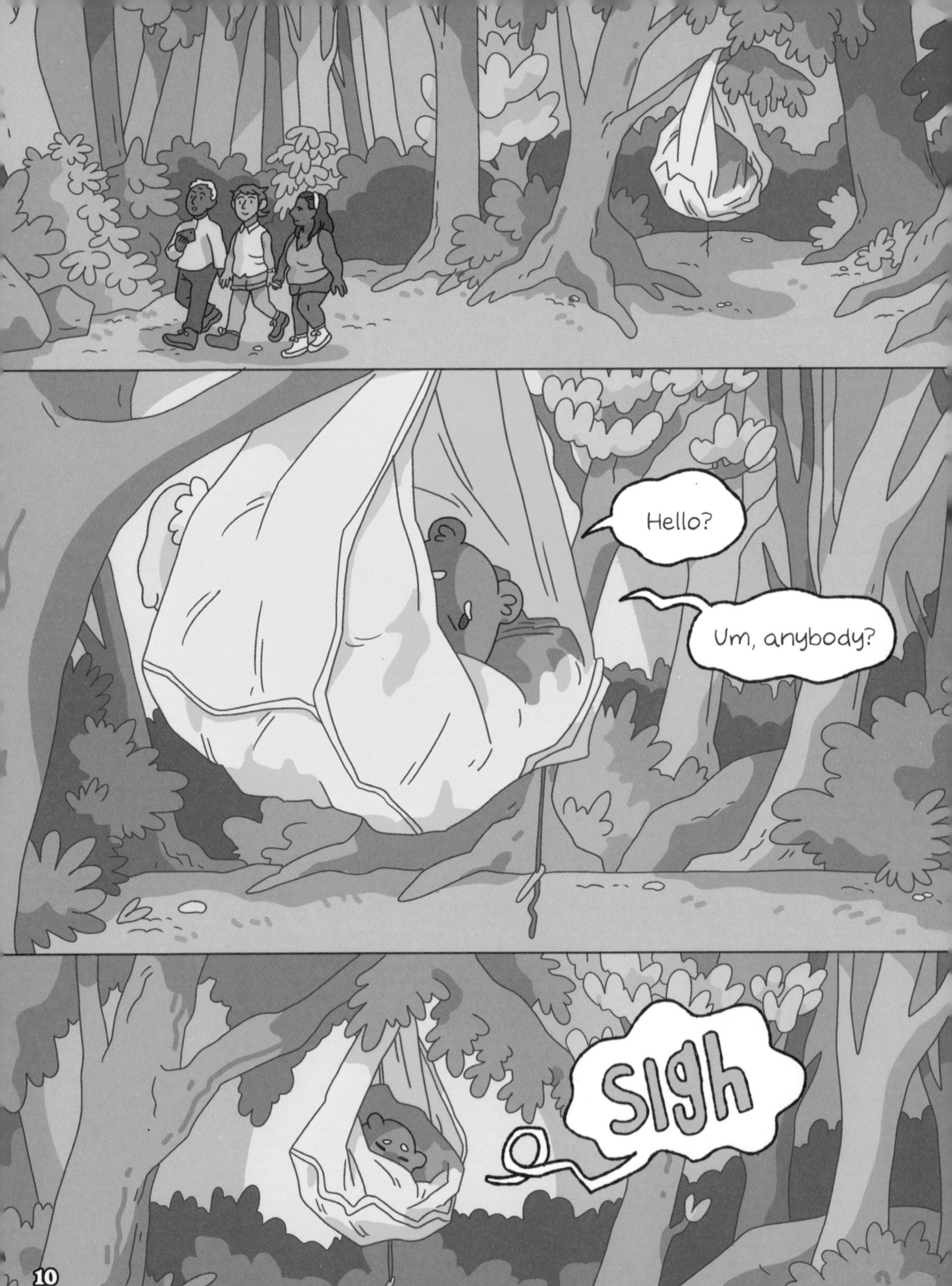
Hello?
Um, anybody?
sigh

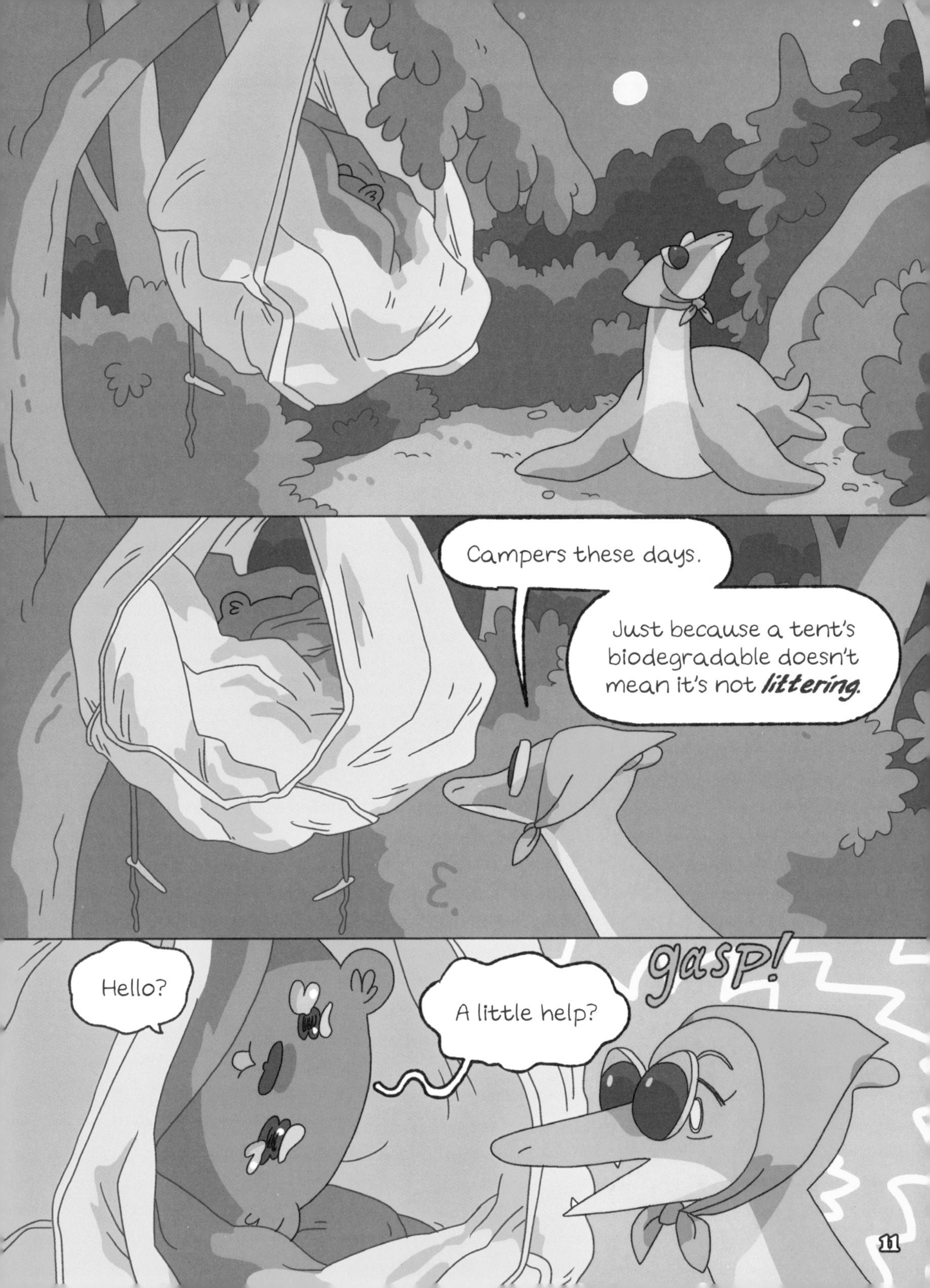
Campers these days.
Just because a tent's biodegradable doesn't mean it's not ***littering***.
Hello?
A little help?
gasp!

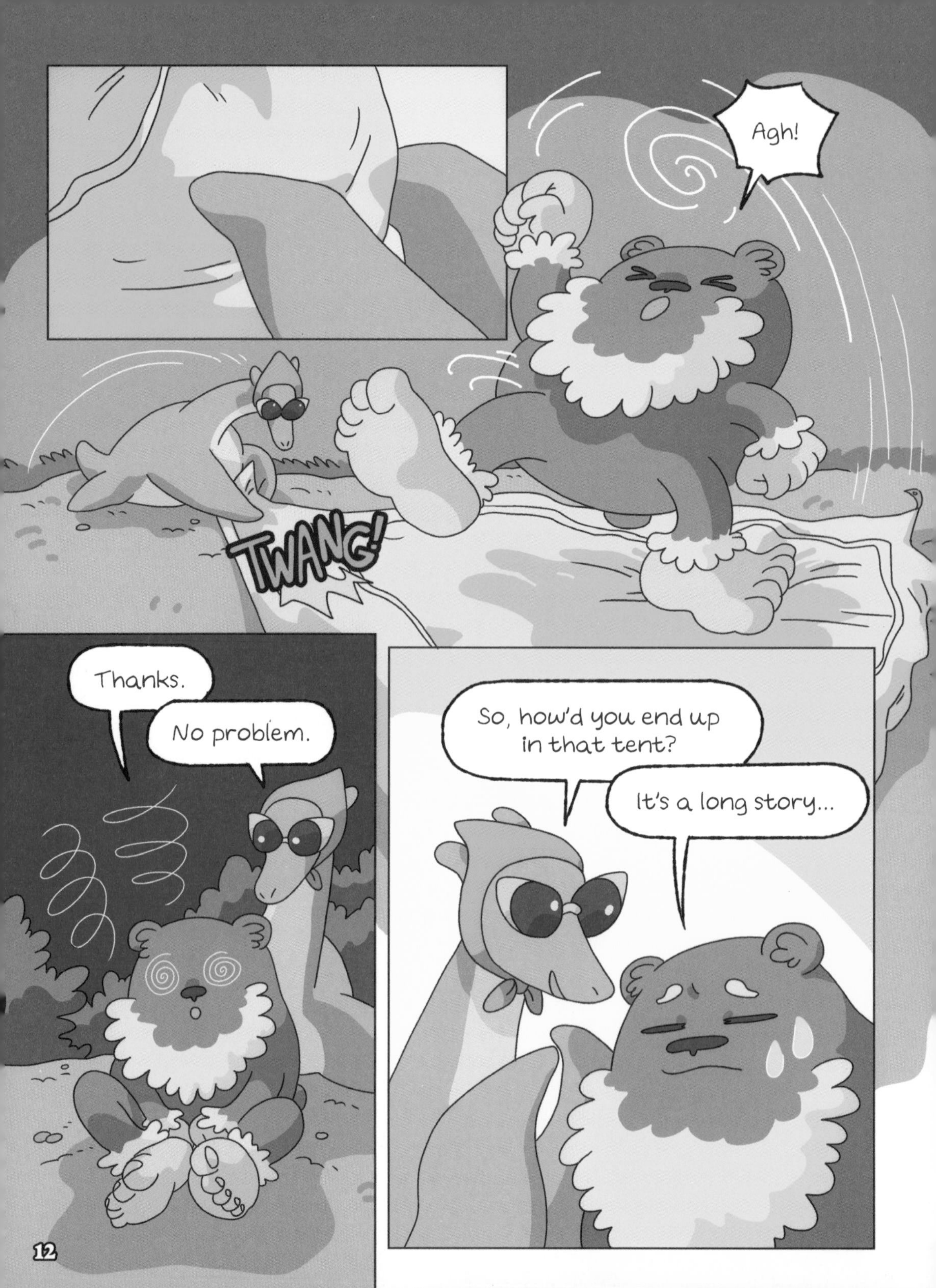
Agh!
TWANG!
Thanks.
No problem.
So, how'd you end up in that tent?
It's a long story...

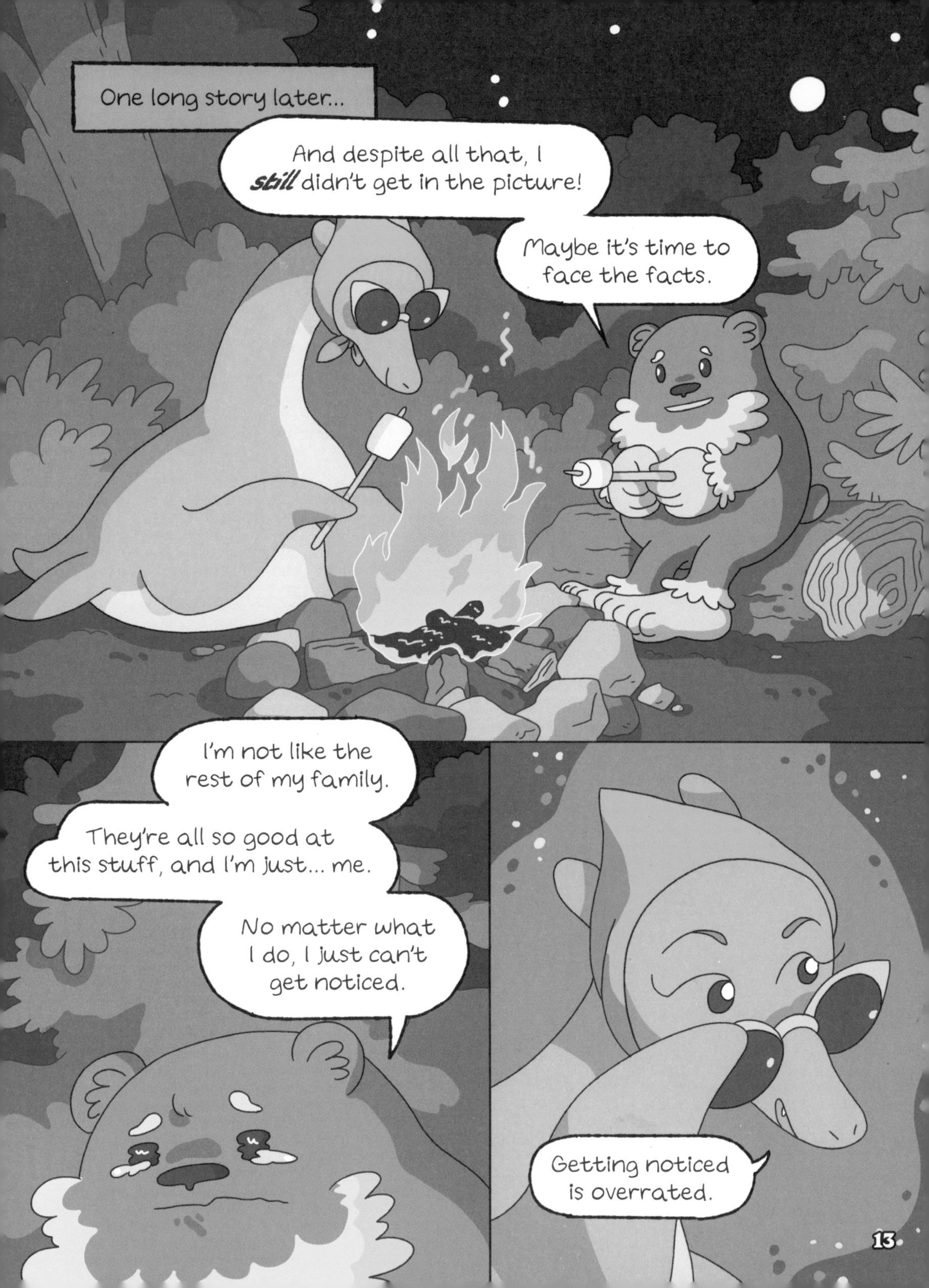
One long story later...
And despite all that, I *still* didn't get in the picture!
Maybe it's time to face the facts.
I'm not like the rest of my family.
They're all so good at this stuff, and I'm just... me.
No matter what I do, I just can't get noticed.
Getting noticed is overrated.

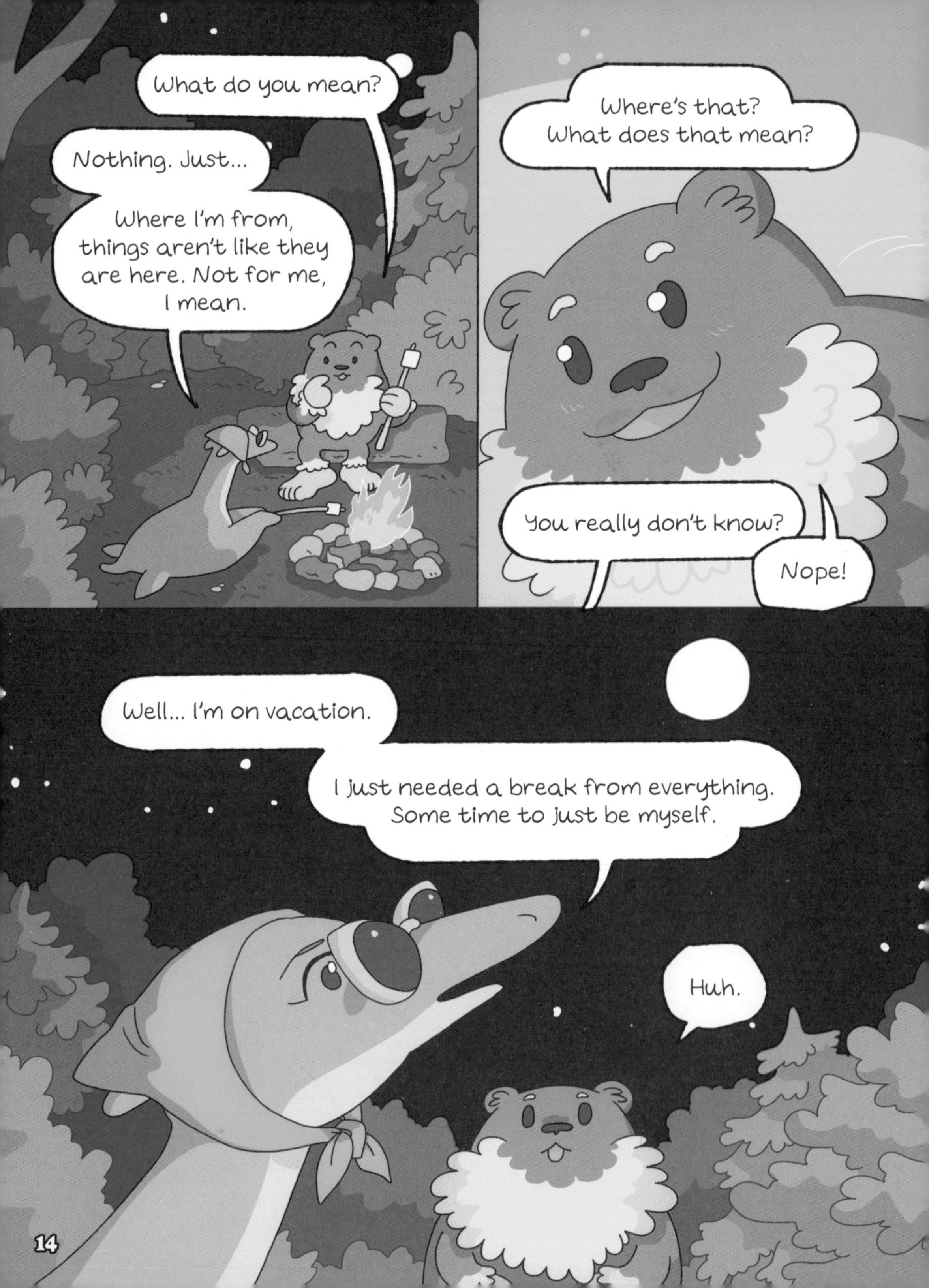
What do you mean?
Nothing. Just...
Where I'm from, things aren't like they are here. Not for me, I mean.
Where's that? What does that mean?
You really don't know?
Nope!
Well... I'm on vacation.
I just needed a break from everything. Some time to just be myself.
Huh.

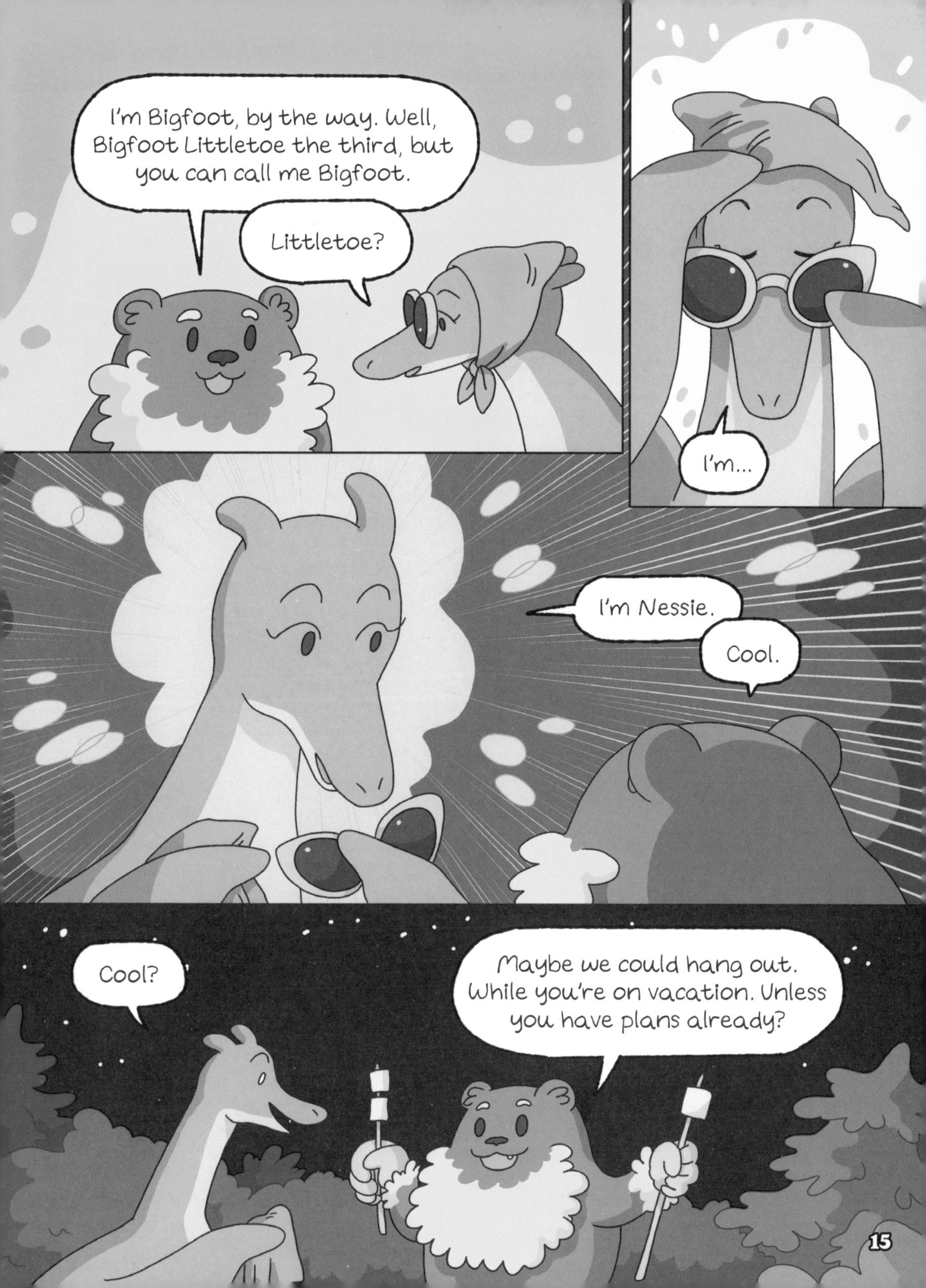
I'm Bigfoot, by the way. Well, Bigfoot Littletoe the third, but you can call me Bigfoot.
Littletoe?
I'm...
I'm Nessie.
Cool.
Cool?
Maybe we could hang out. While you're on vacation. Unless you have plans already?

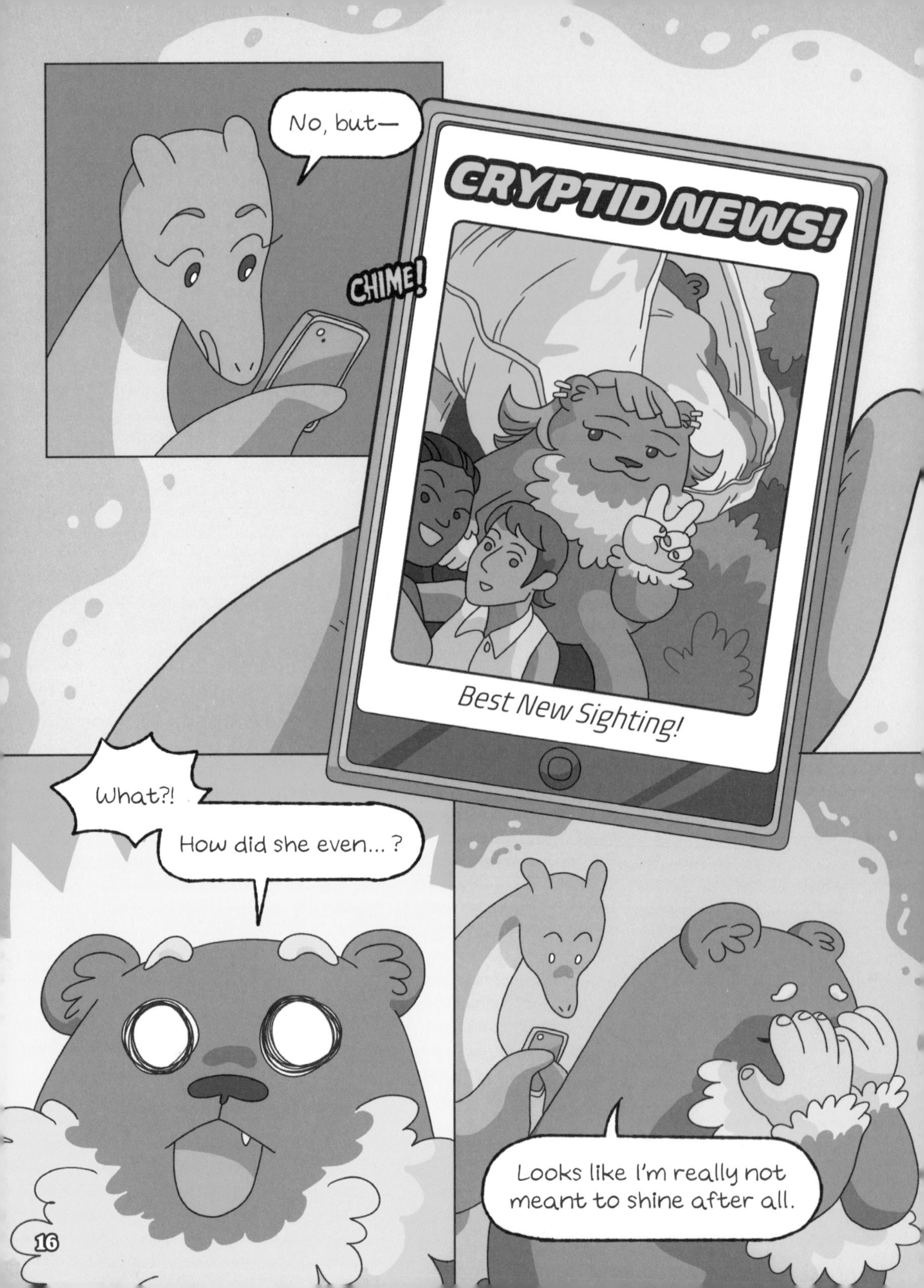
No, but—
CHIME!
CRYPTID NEWS!
Best New Sighting!
What?!
How did she even... ?
Looks like I'm really not meant to shine after all.

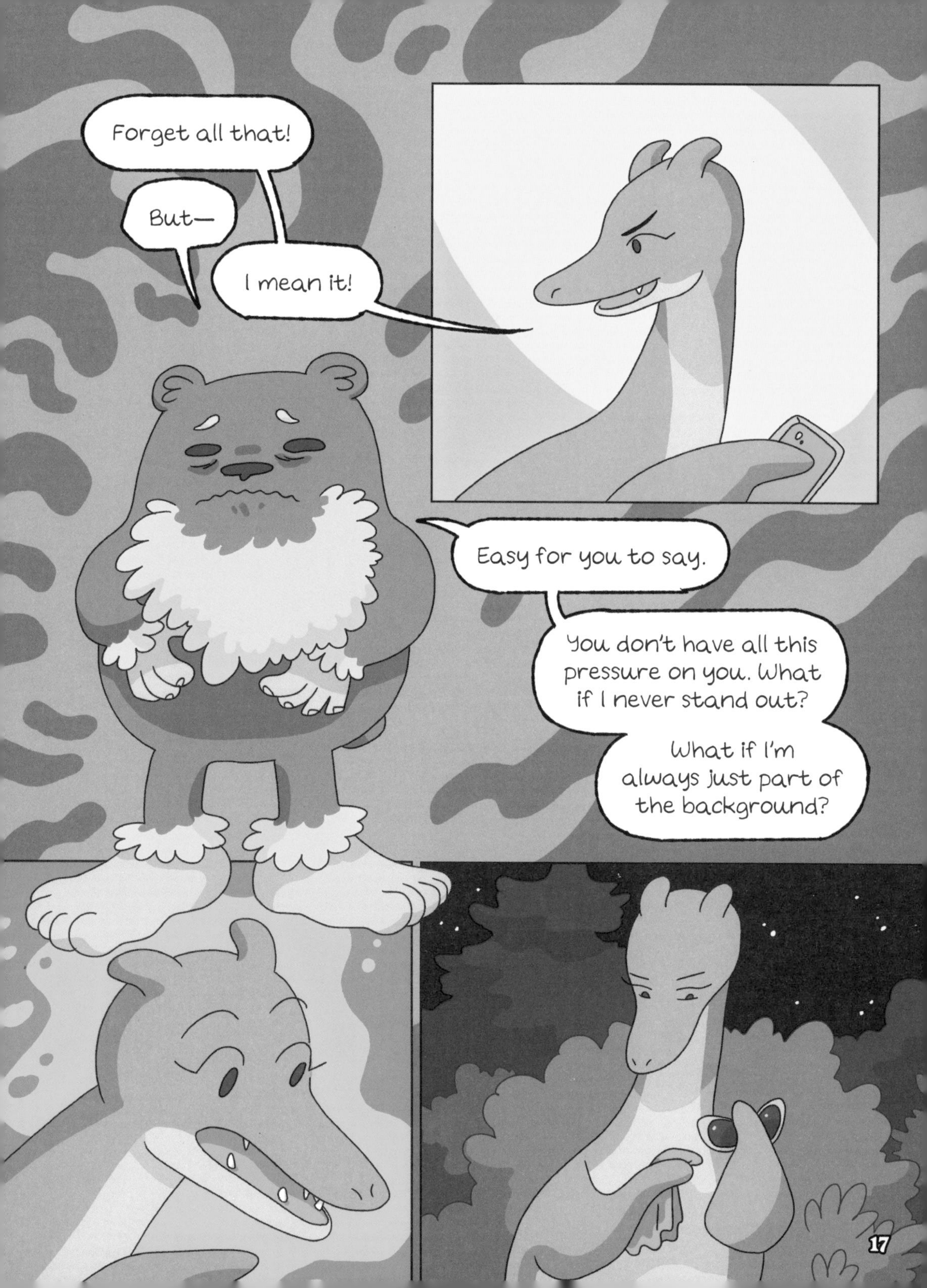
Forget all that!
But—
I mean it!
Easy for you to say.
You don't have all this pressure on you. What if I never stand out?
What if I'm always just part of the background?

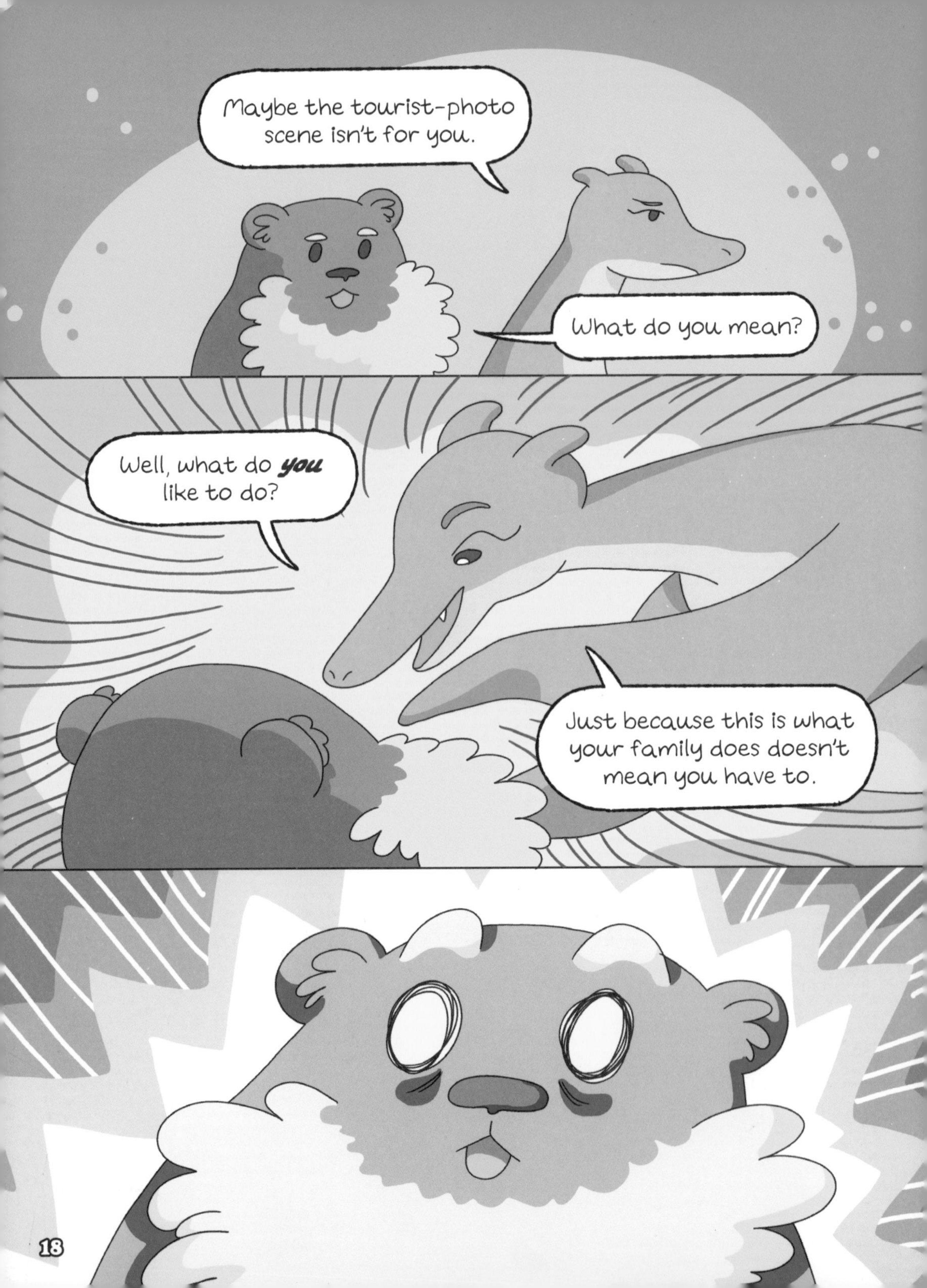
Maybe the tourist-photo scene isn't for you.
What do you mean?
Well, what do ***you*** like to do?
Just because this is what your family does doesn't mean you have to.

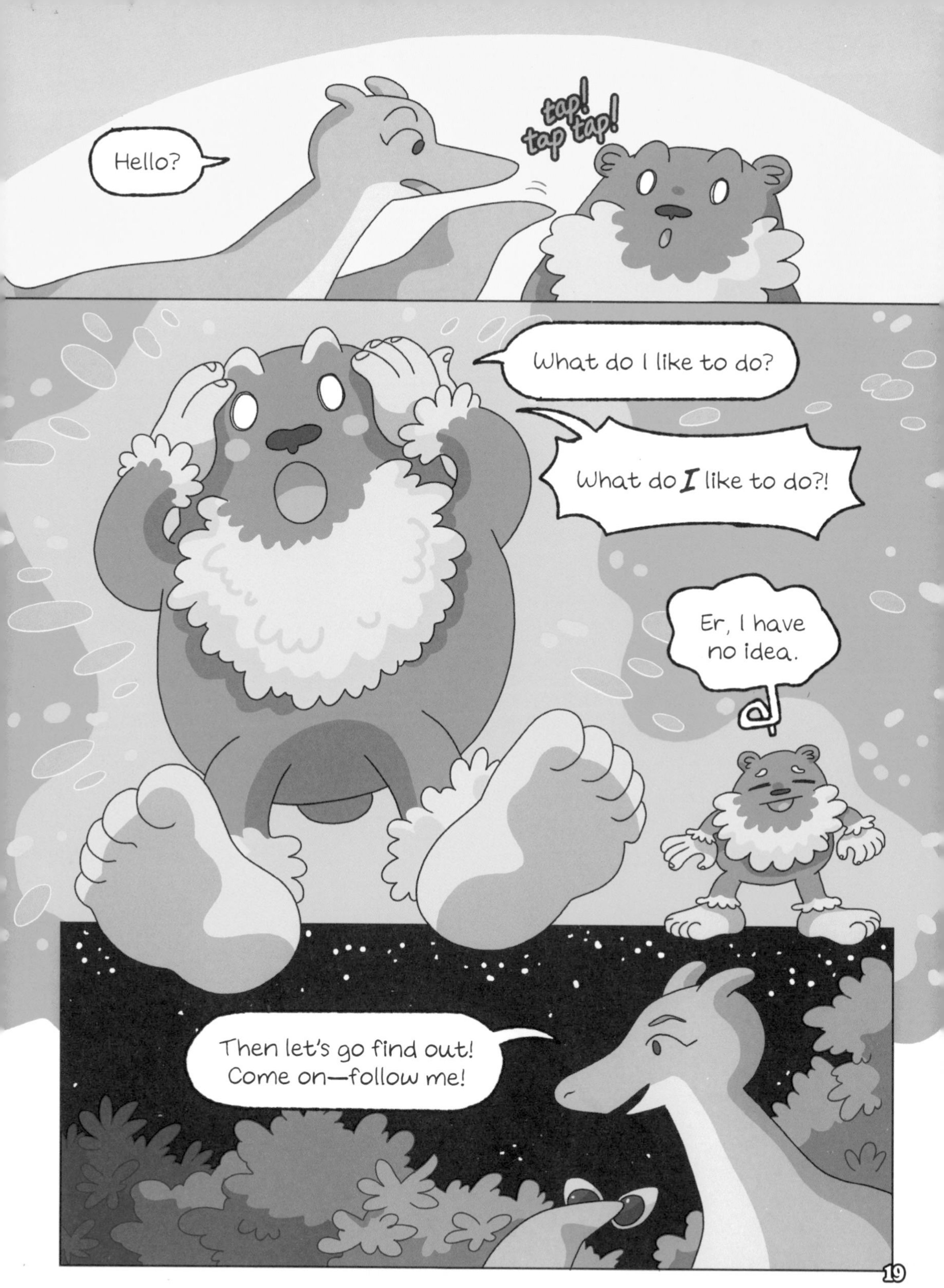
Hello?
tap! tap tap!
What do I like to do?
What do I like to do?!
Er, I have no idea.
Then let's go find out! Come on—follow me!

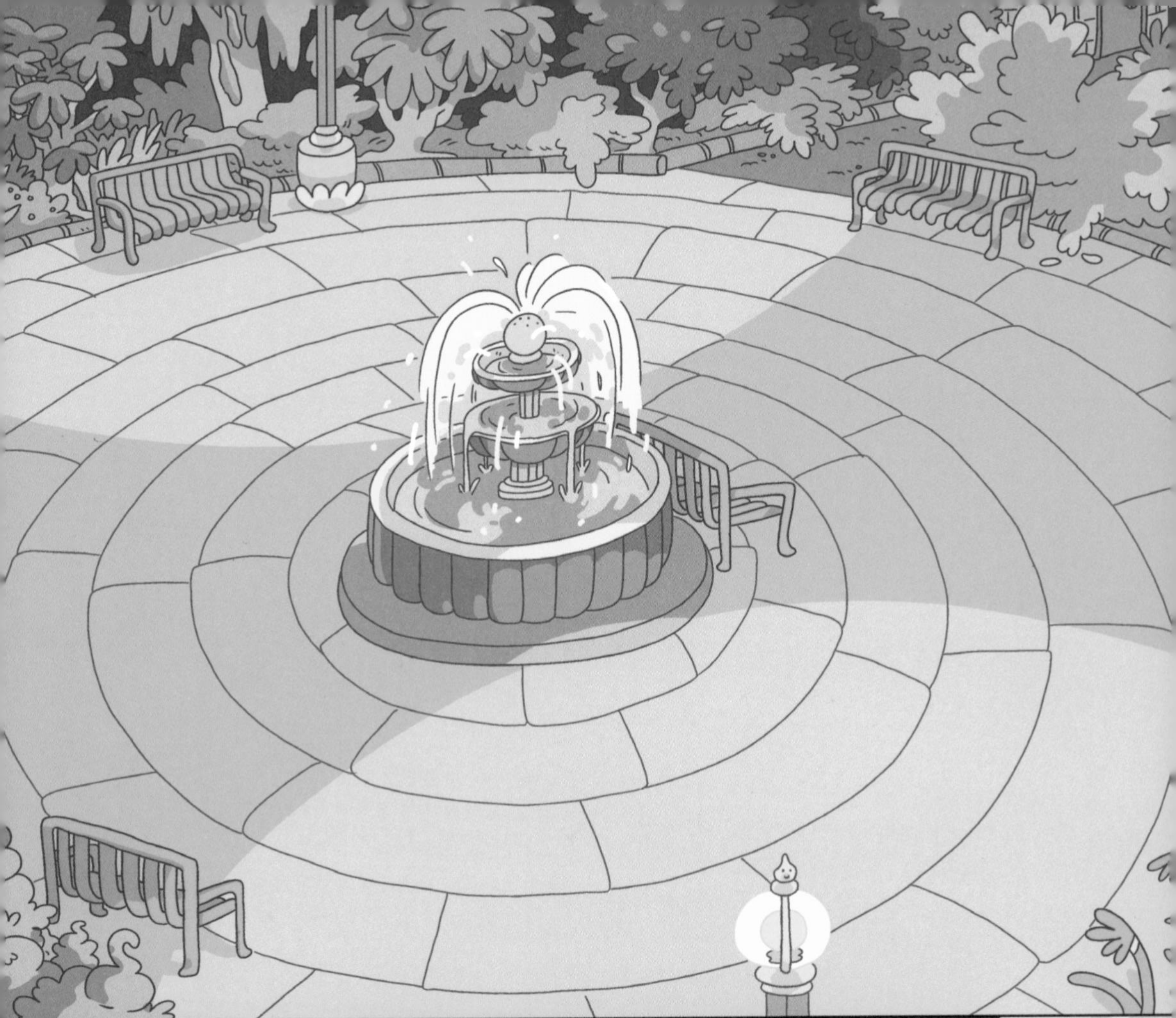

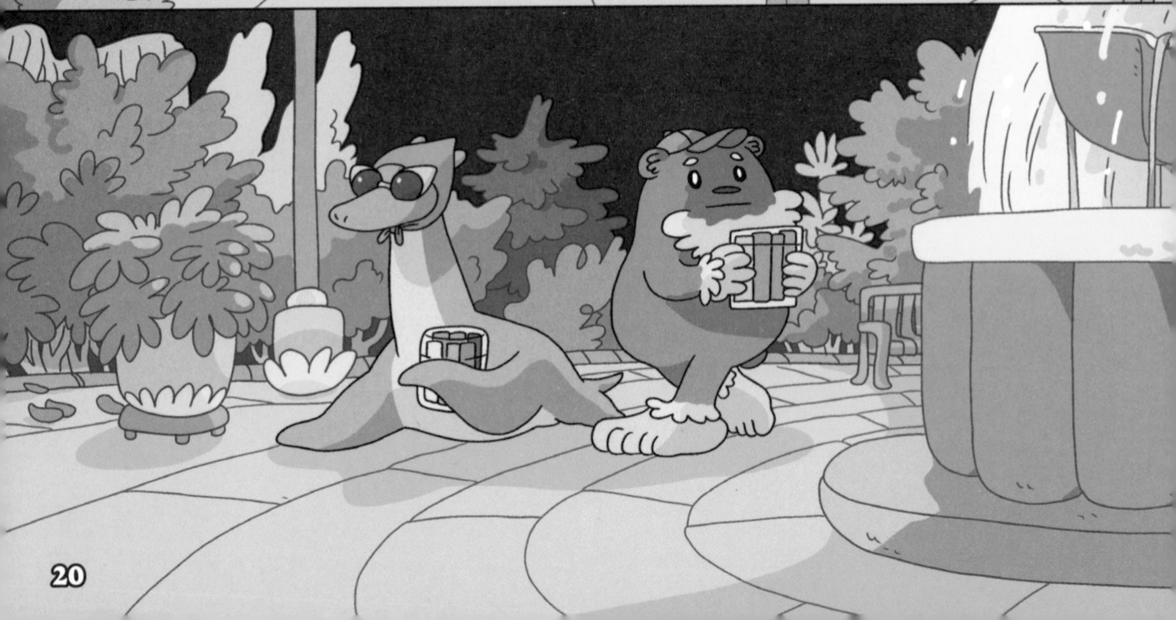

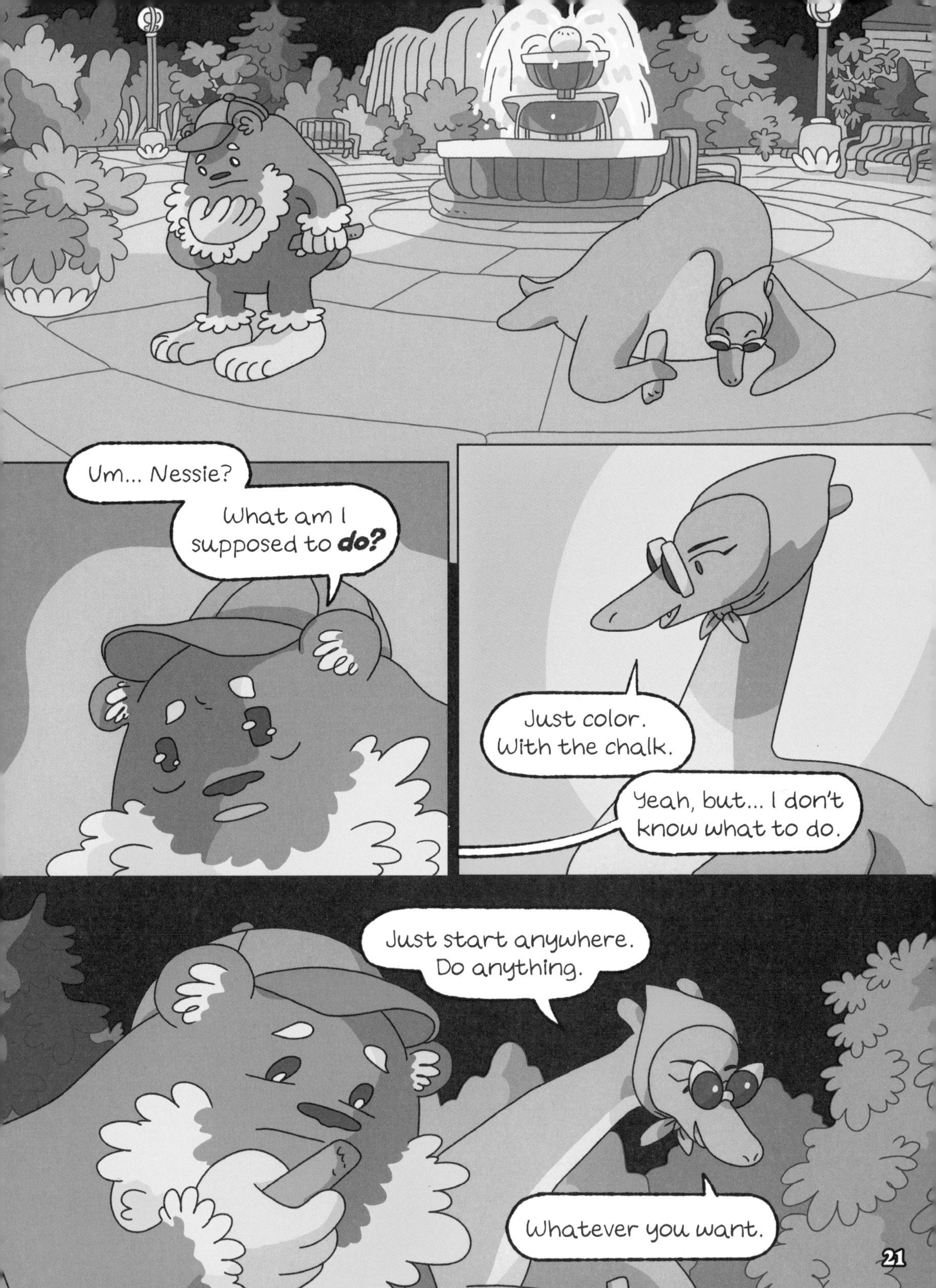
Um... Nessie?
What am I supposed to **do?**
Just color. With the chalk.
Yeah, but... I don't know what to do.
Just start anywhere. Do anything.
Whatever you want.

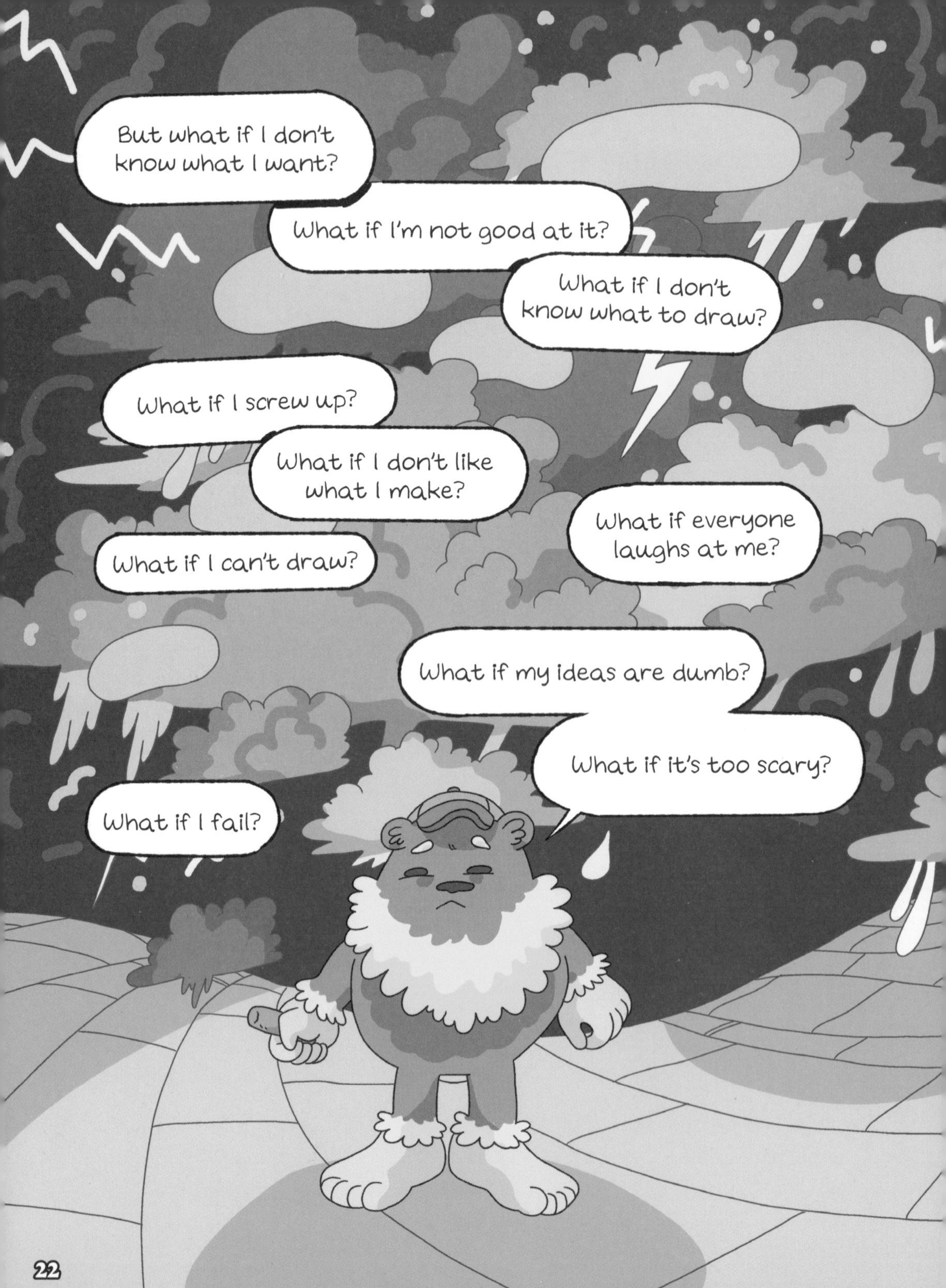
But what if I don't know what I want?
What if I'm not good at it?
What if I don't know what to draw?
What if I screw up?
What if I don't like what I make?
What if everyone laughs at me?
What if I can't draw?
What if my ideas are dumb?
What if it's too scary?
What if I fail?

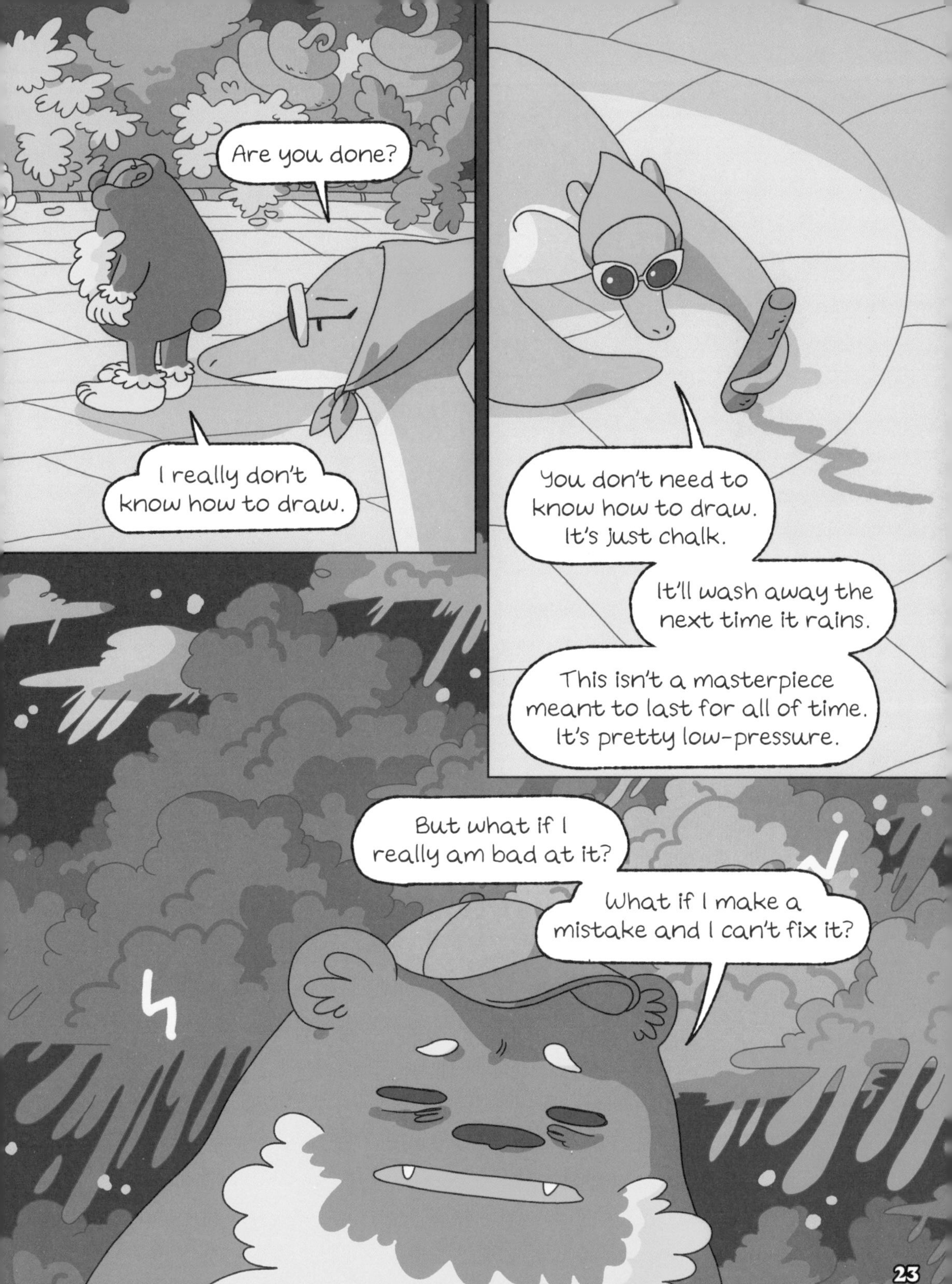
Are you done?
I really don't know how to draw.
You don't need to know how to draw. It's just chalk.
It'll wash away the next time it rains.
This isn't a masterpiece meant to last for all of time. It's pretty low-pressure.
But what if I really am bad at it?
What if I make a mistake and I can't fix it?

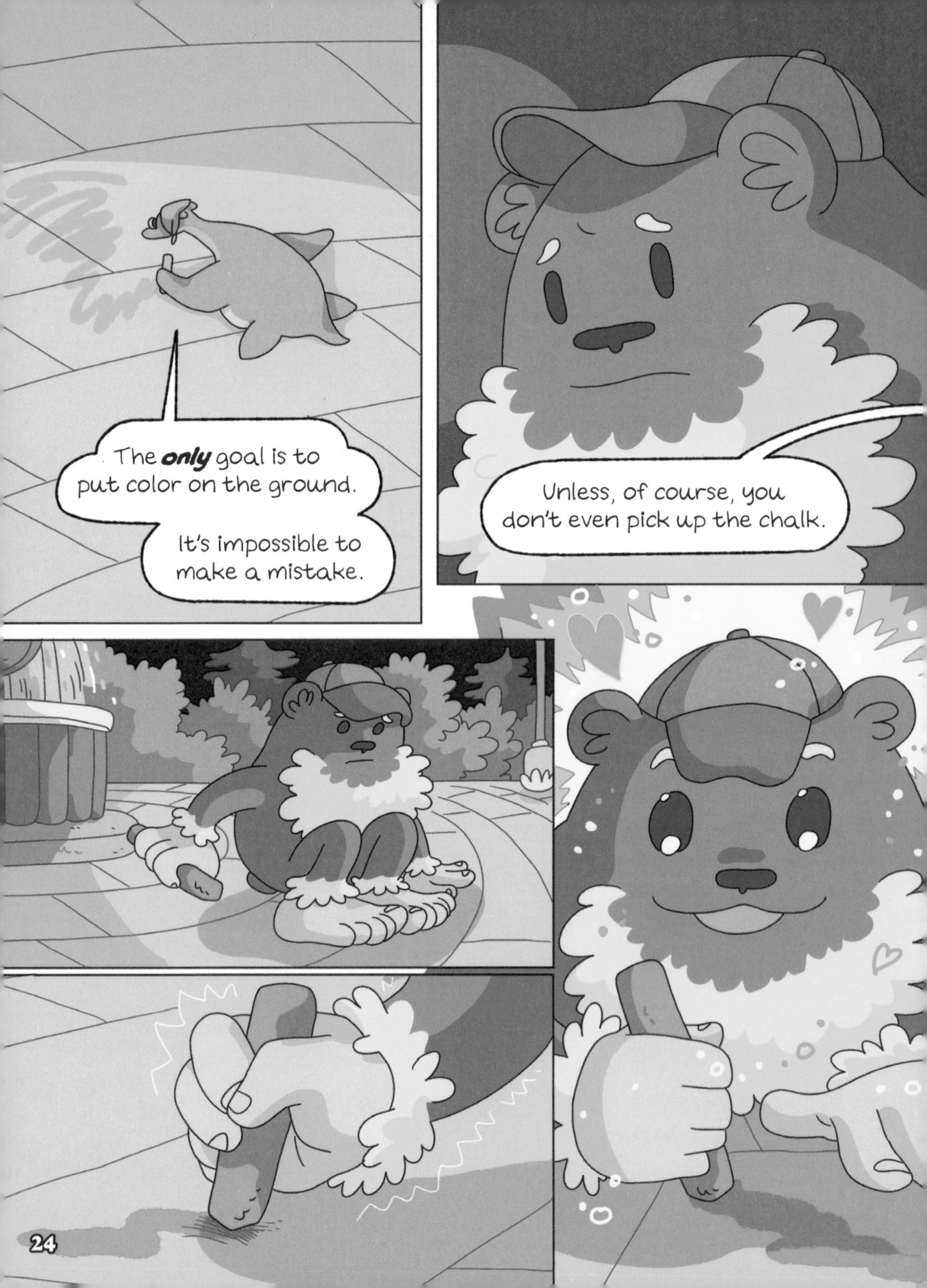

The **only** goal is to put color on the ground.
It's impossible to make a mistake.
Unless, of course, you don't even pick up the chalk.

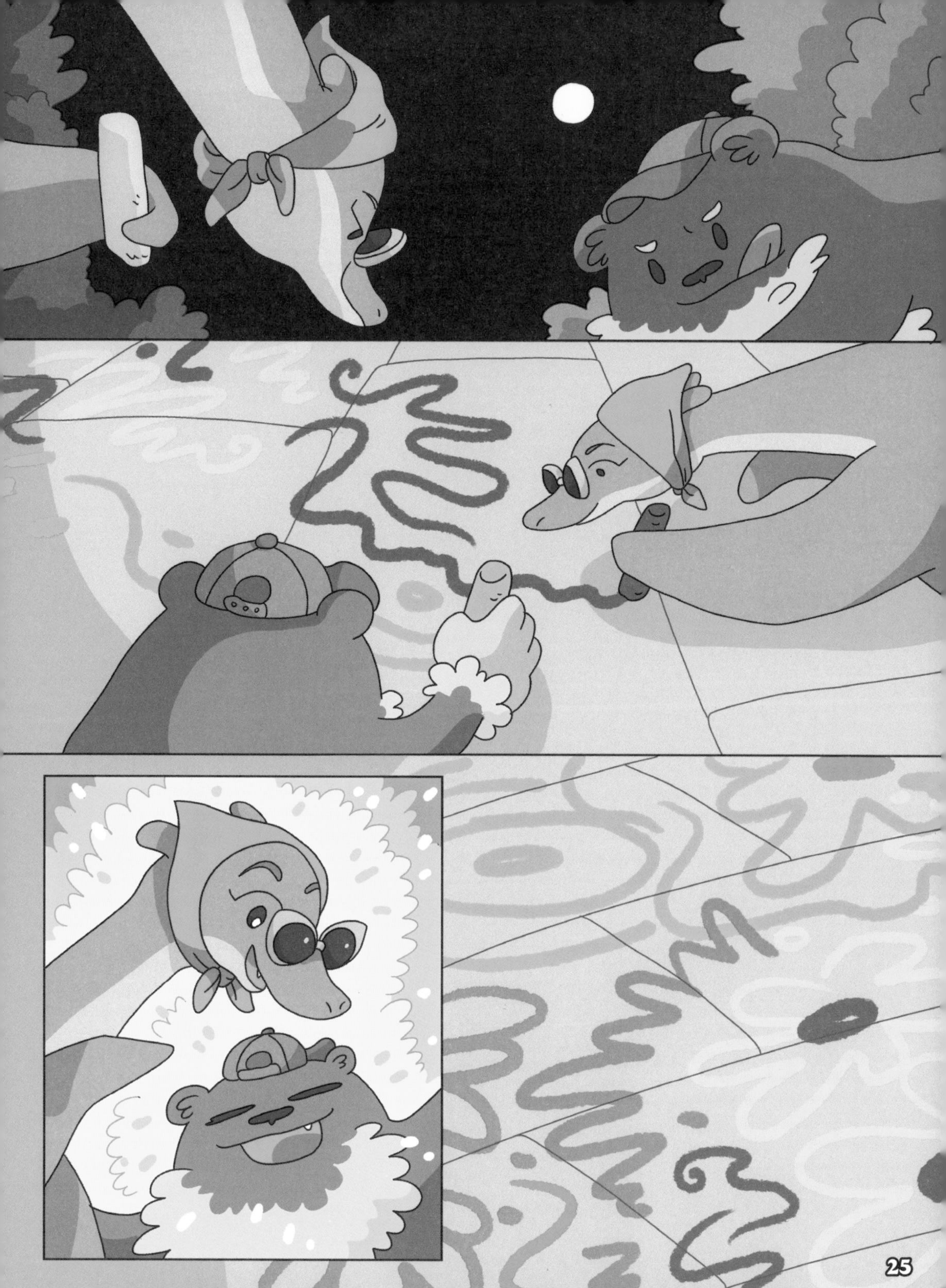

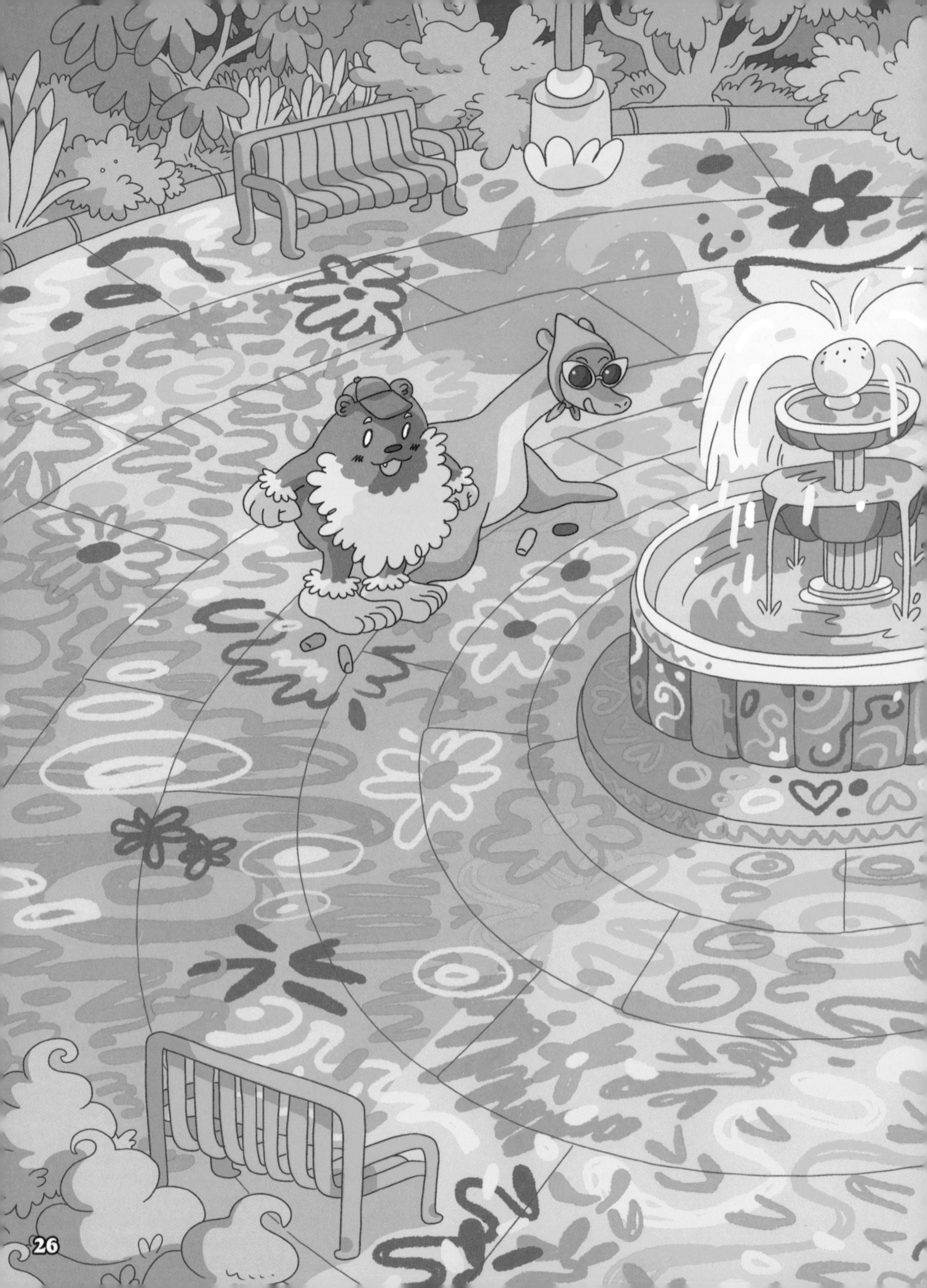

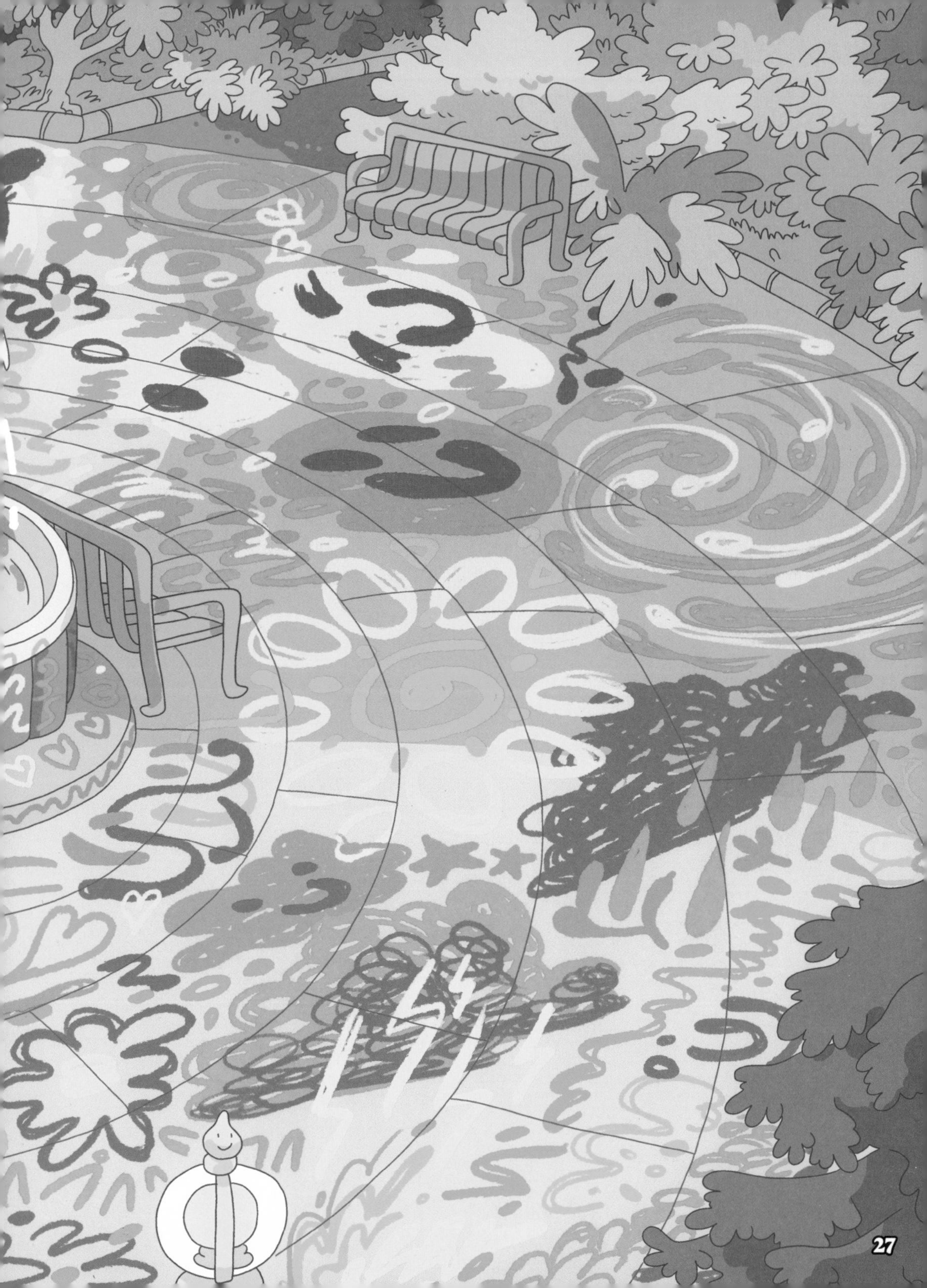

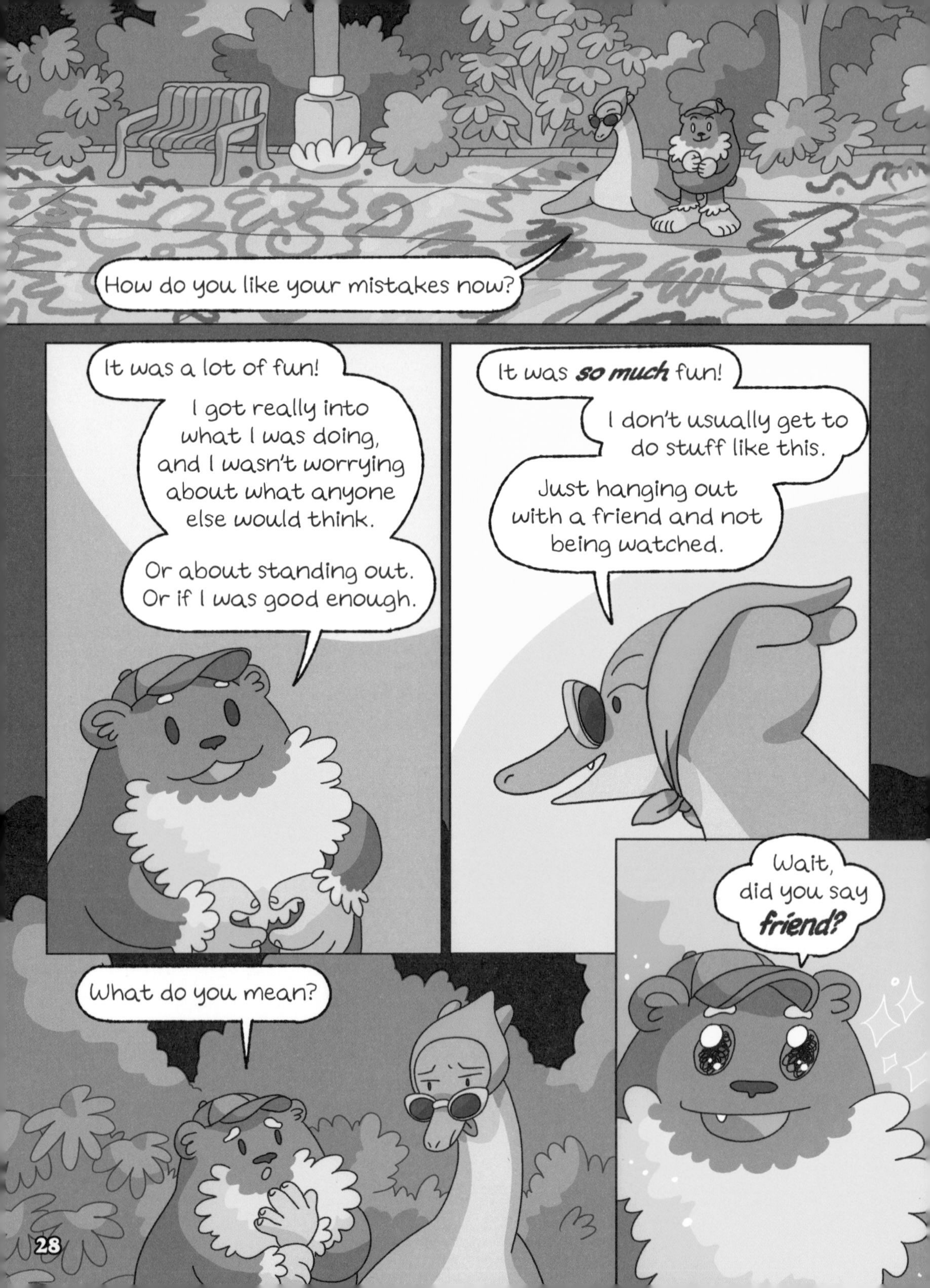
How do you like your mistakes now?
It was a lot of fun!
I got really into what I was doing, and I wasn't worrying about what anyone else would think.
Or about standing out. Or if I was good enough.
It was **so much** fun!
I don't usually get to do stuff like this.
Just hanging out with a friend and not being watched.
Wait, did you say **friend?**
What do you mean?

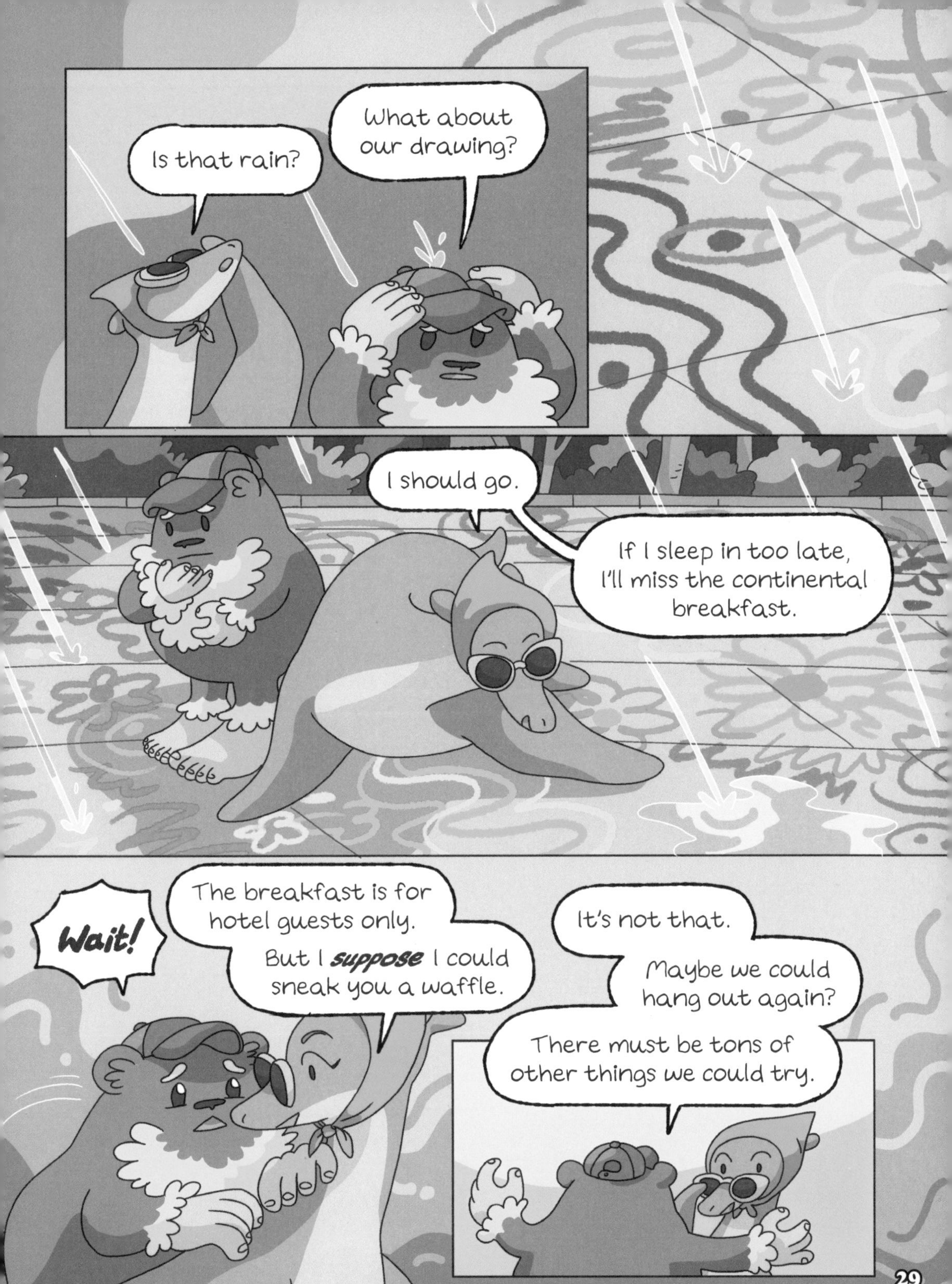
Is that rain?
What about our drawing?
I should go.
If I sleep in too late, I'll miss the continental breakfast.
Wait!
The breakfast is for hotel guests only.
But I *suppose* I could sneak you a waffle.
It's not that.
Maybe we could hang out again?
There must be tons of other things we could try.

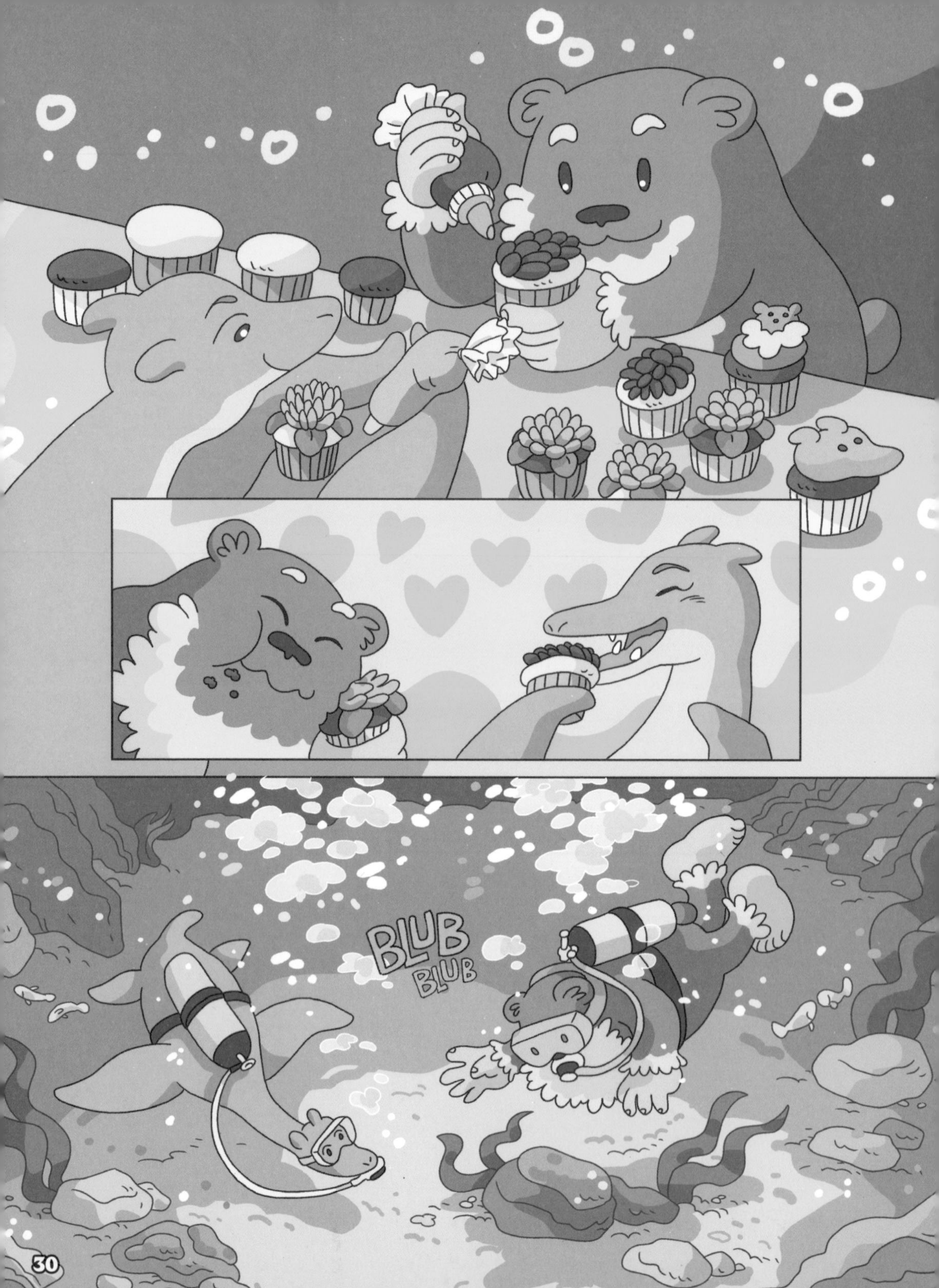
BLUB
BLUB

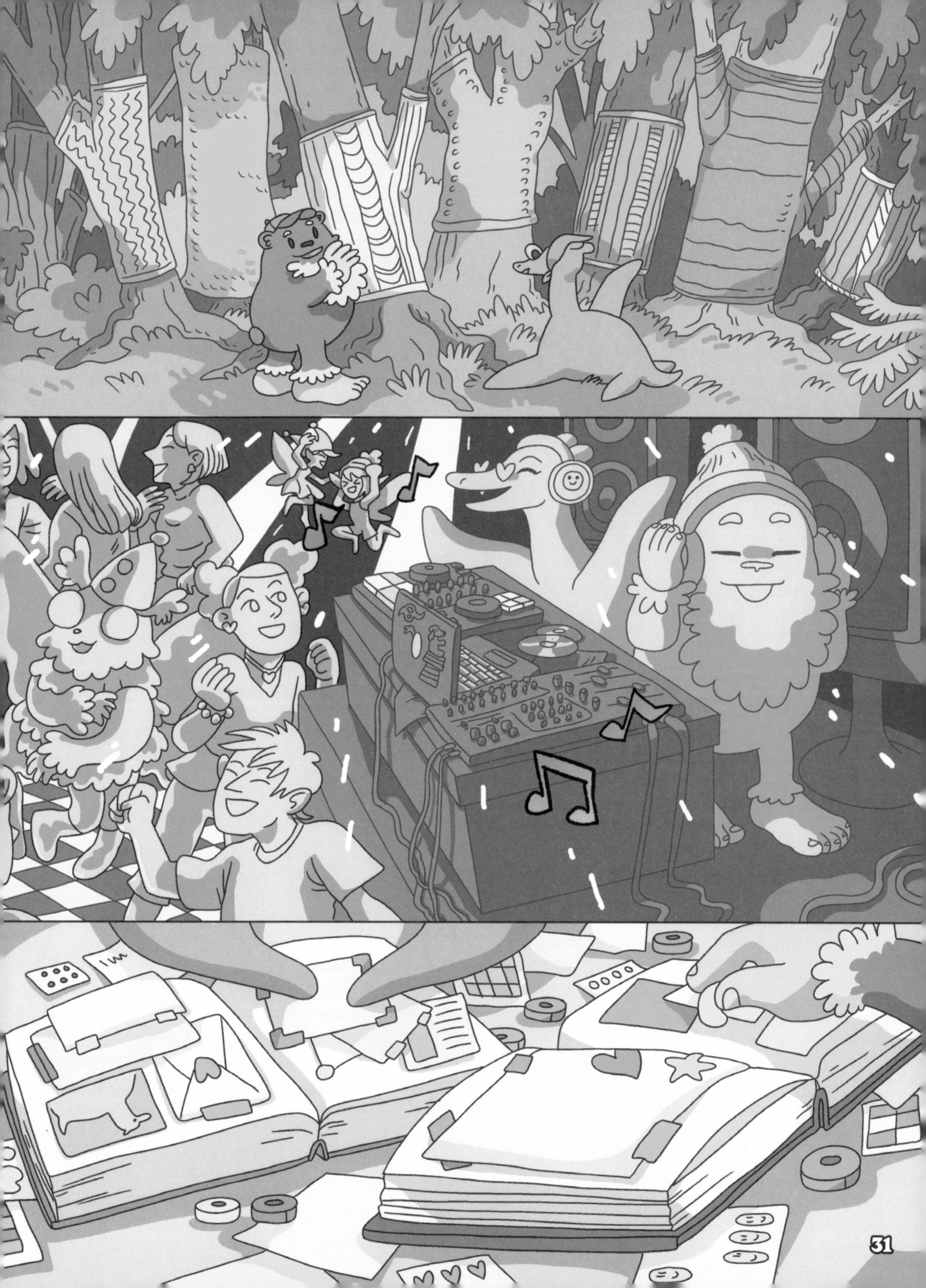

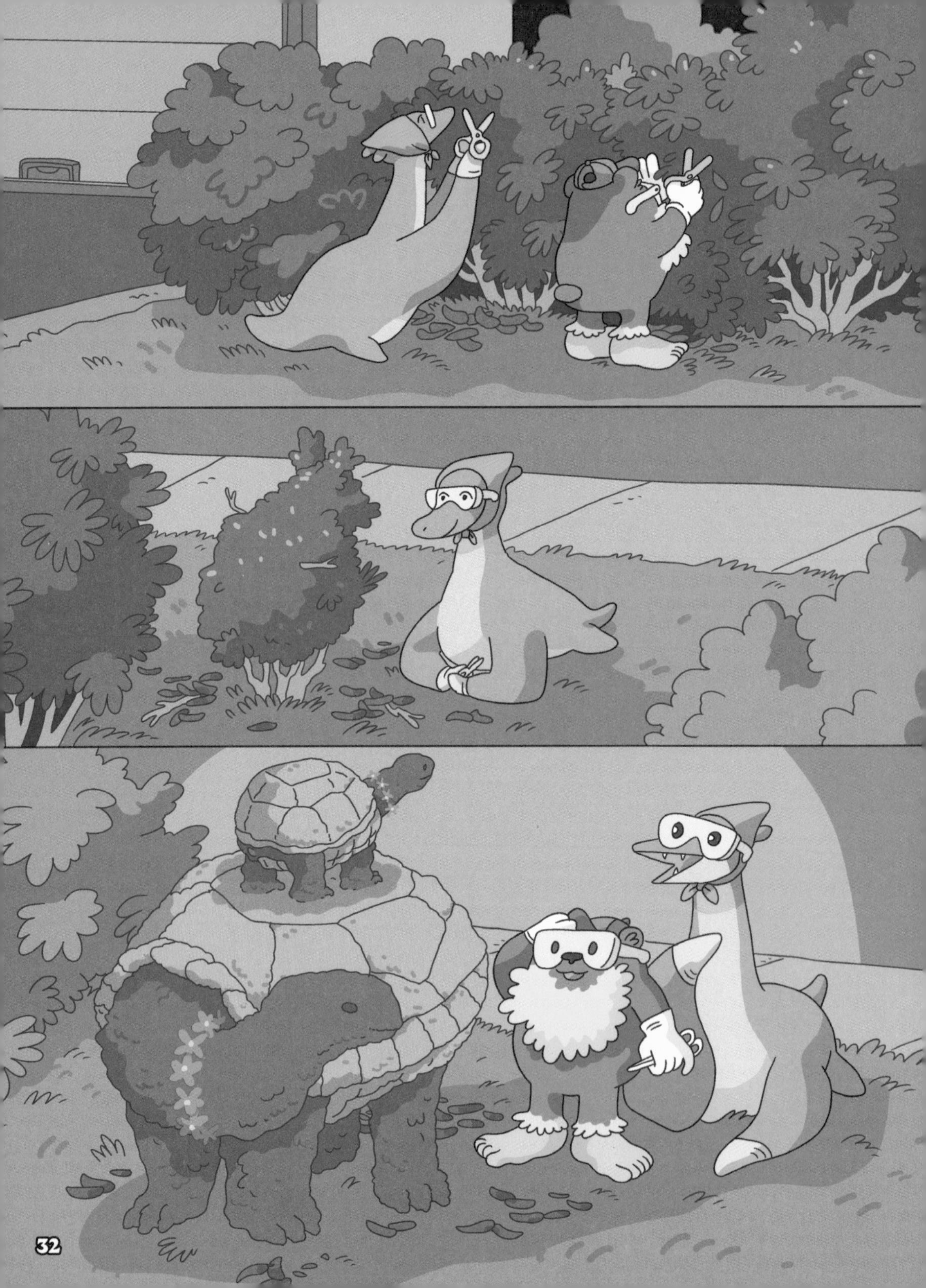

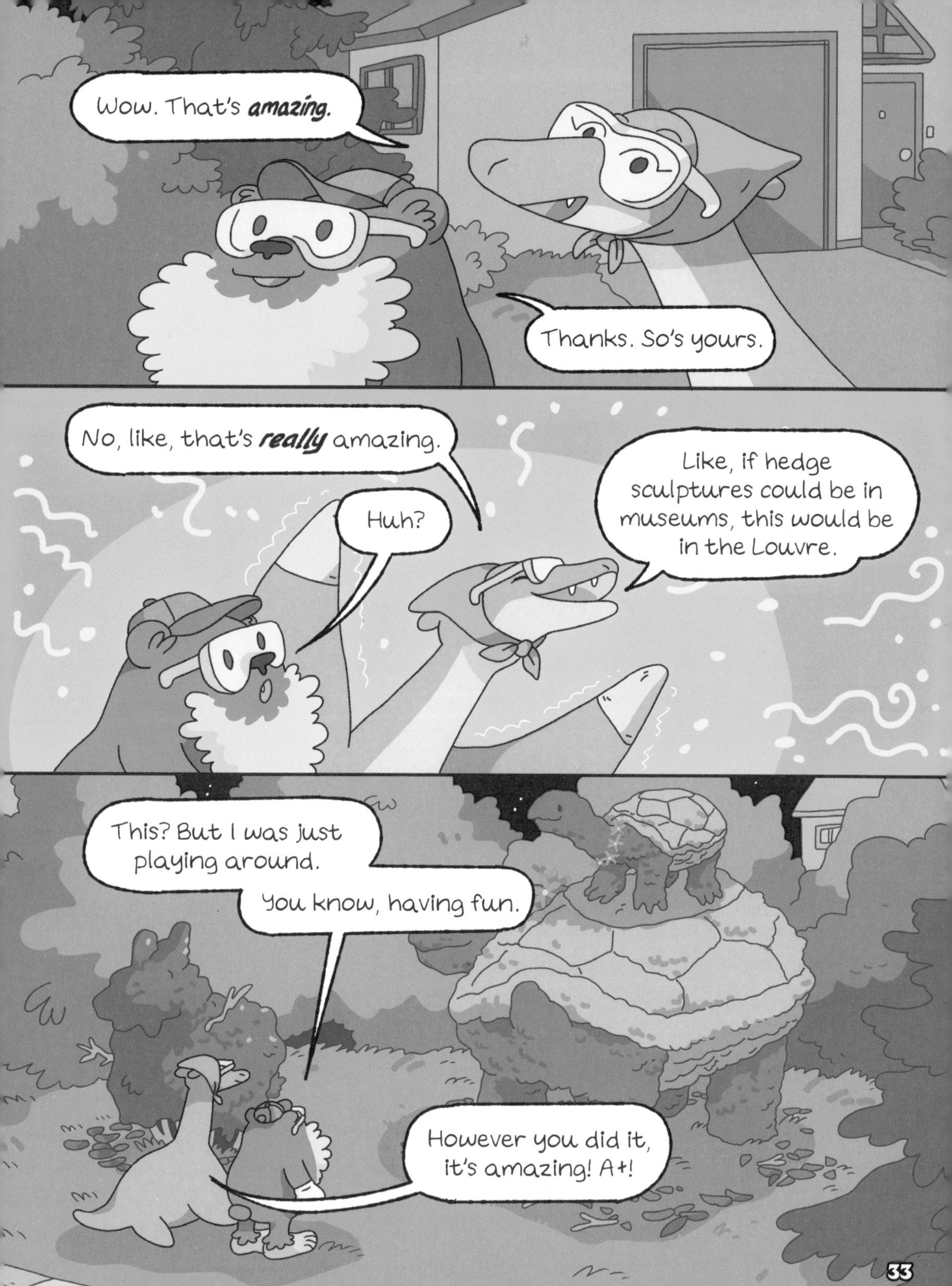
Wow. That's ***amazing.***
Thanks. So's yours.
No, like, that's ***really*** amazing.
Huh?
Like, if hedge sculptures could be in museums, this would be in the Louvre.
This? But I was just playing around.
You know, having fun.
However you did it, it's amazing! A+!

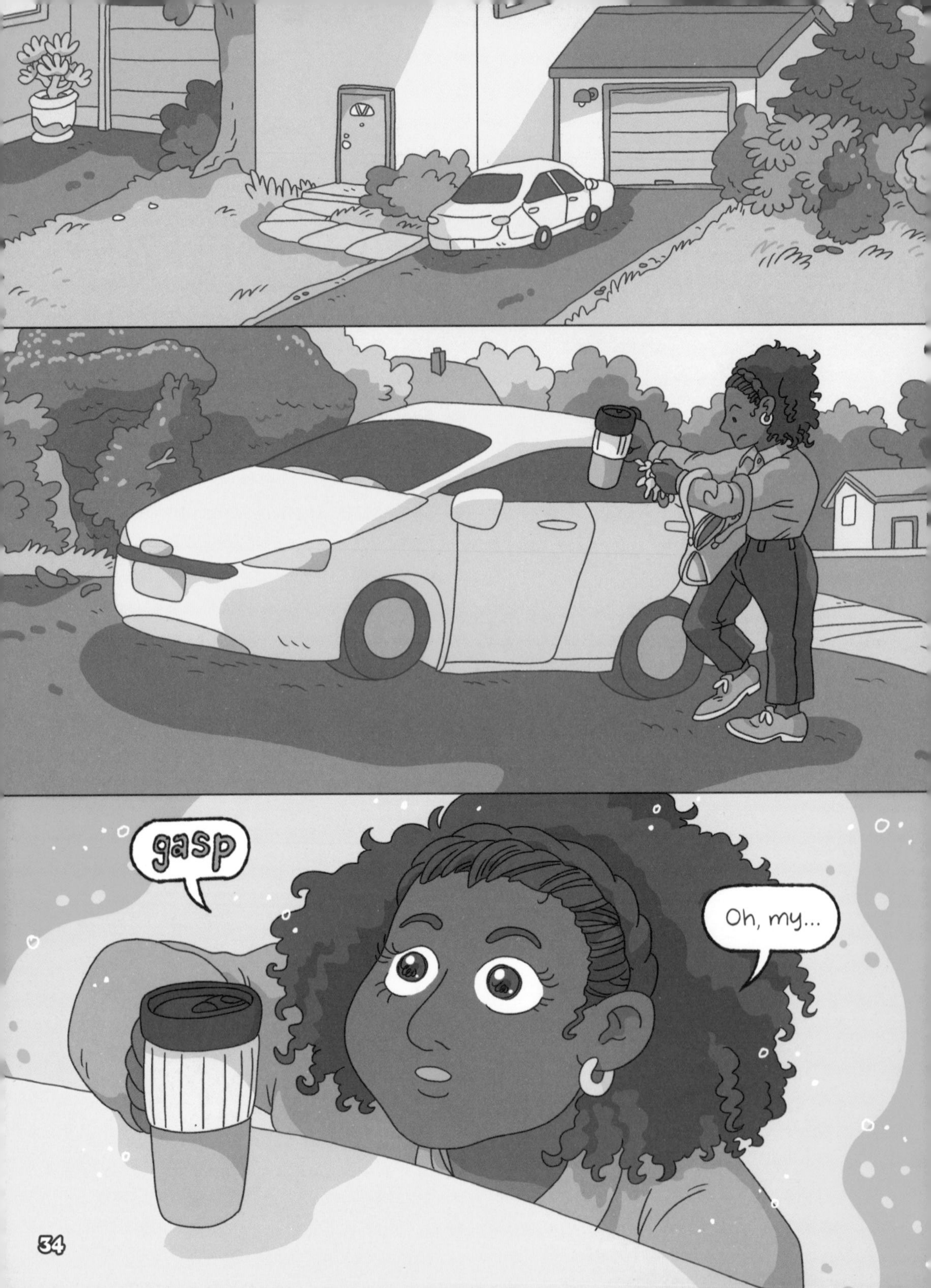
gasp
Oh, my...

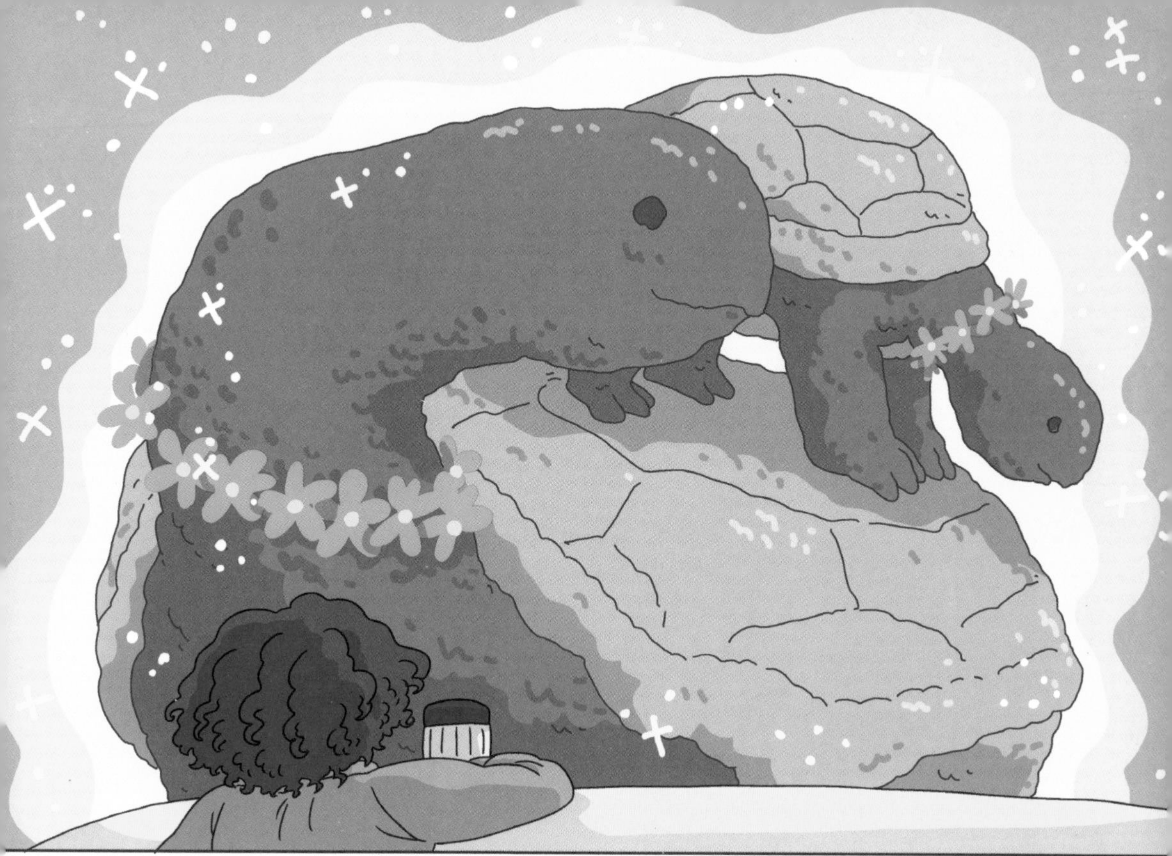

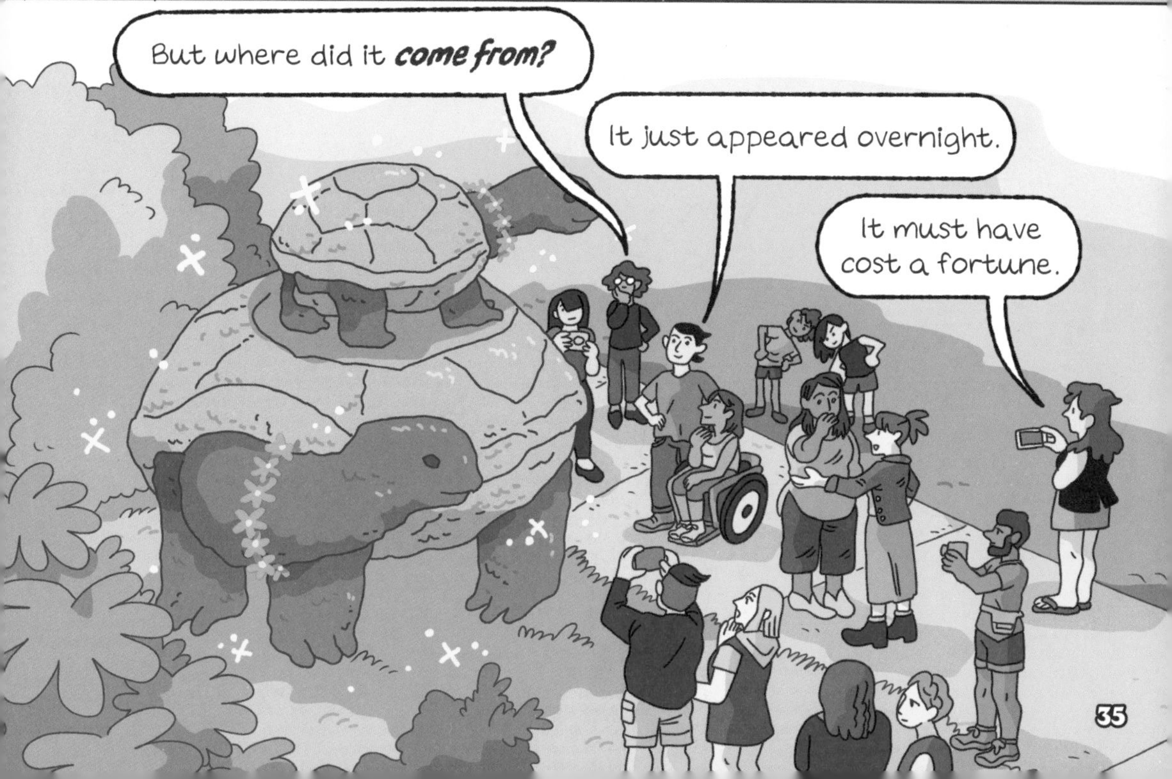

But where did it **come from?**
It just appeared overnight.
It must have cost a fortune.

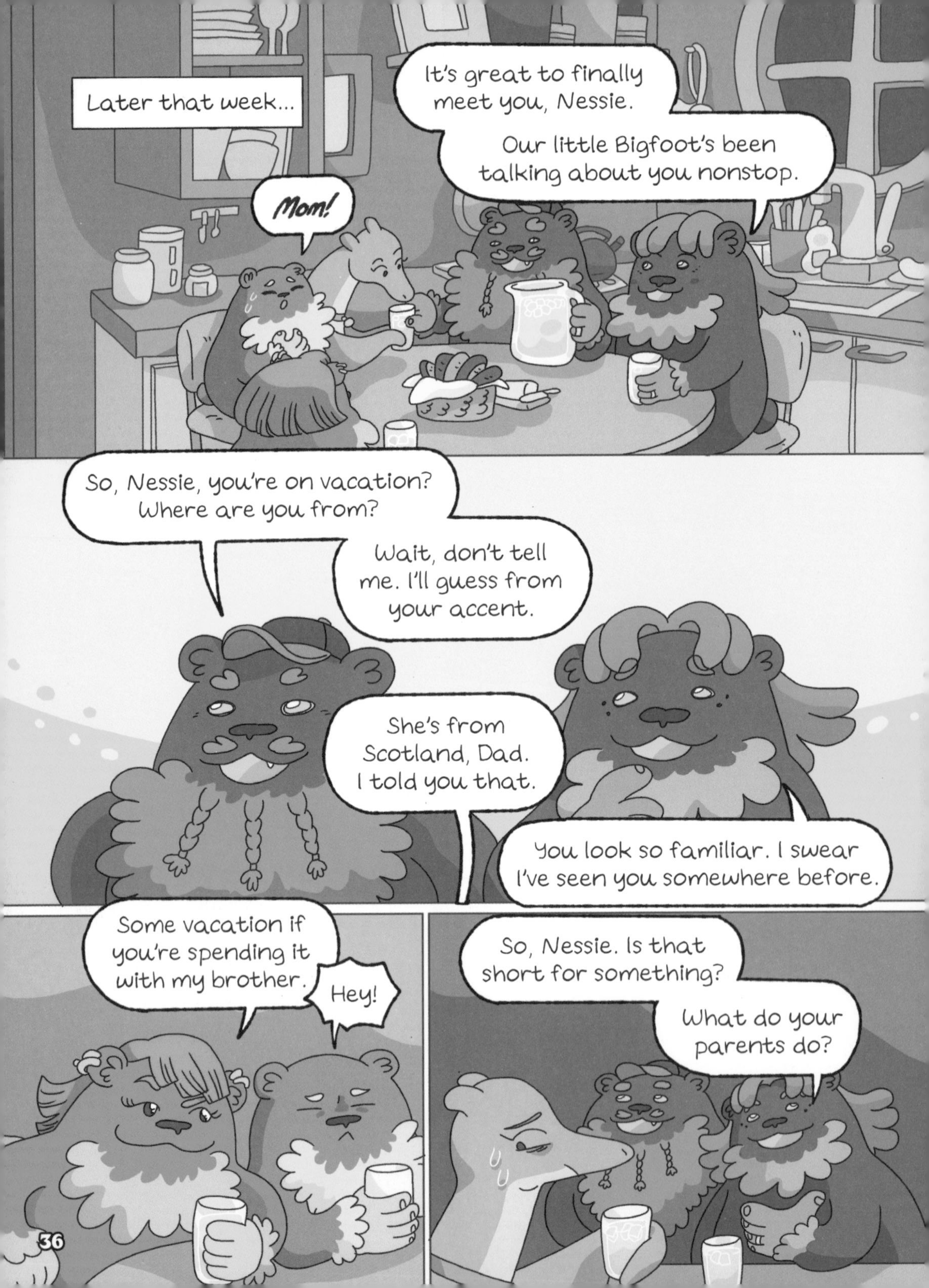

Later that week...
It's great to finally meet you, Nessie.
Our little Bigfoot's been talking about you nonstop.
Mom!
So, Nessie, you're on vacation? Where are you from?
Wait, don't tell me. I'll guess from your accent.
She's from Scotland, Dad. I told you that.
You look so familiar. I swear I've seen you somewhere before.
Some vacation if you're spending it with my brother.
Hey!
So, Nessie. Is that short for something?
What do your parents do?

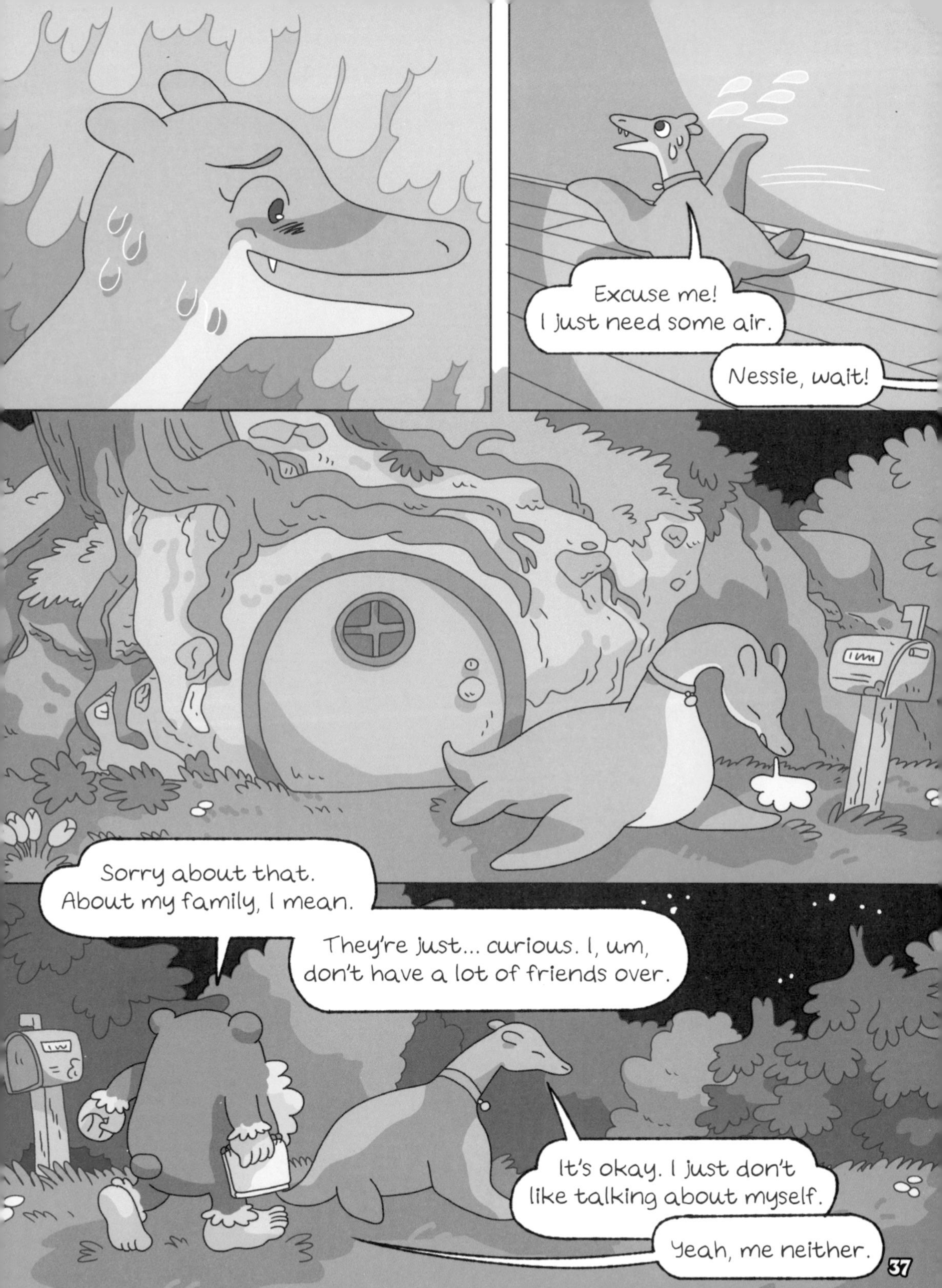
Excuse me!
I just need some air.
Nessie, wait!
Sorry about that.
About my family, I mean.
They're just... curious. I, um,
don't have a lot of friends over.
It's okay. I just don't
like talking about myself.
Yeah, me neither.

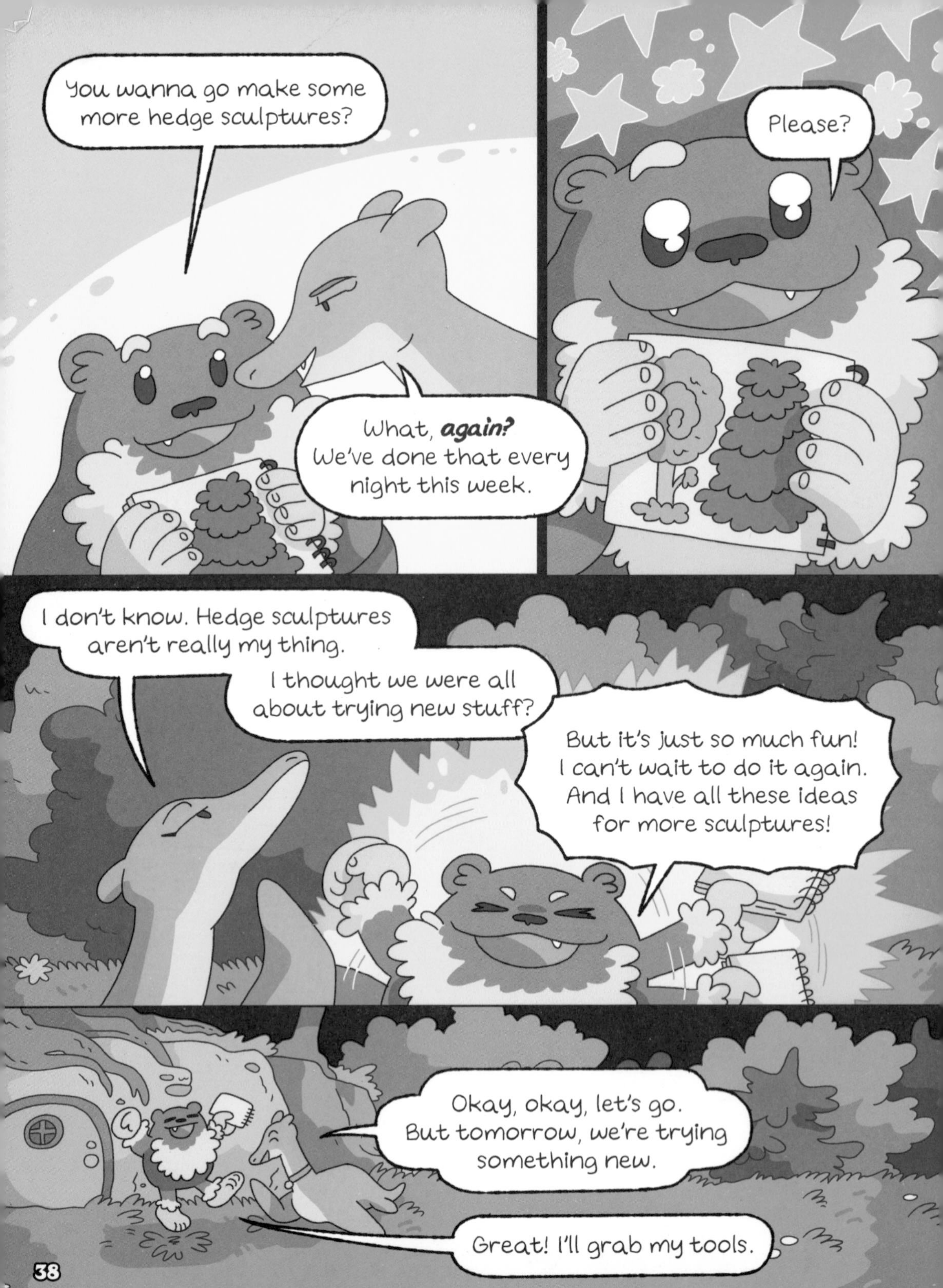
You wanna go make some more hedge sculptures?
What, ***again?*** We've done that every night this week.
Please?
I don't know. Hedge sculptures aren't really my thing.
I thought we were all about trying new stuff?
But it's just so much fun! I can't wait to do it again. And I have all these ideas for more sculptures!
Okay, okay, let's go. But tomorrow, we're trying something new.
Great! I'll grab my tools.

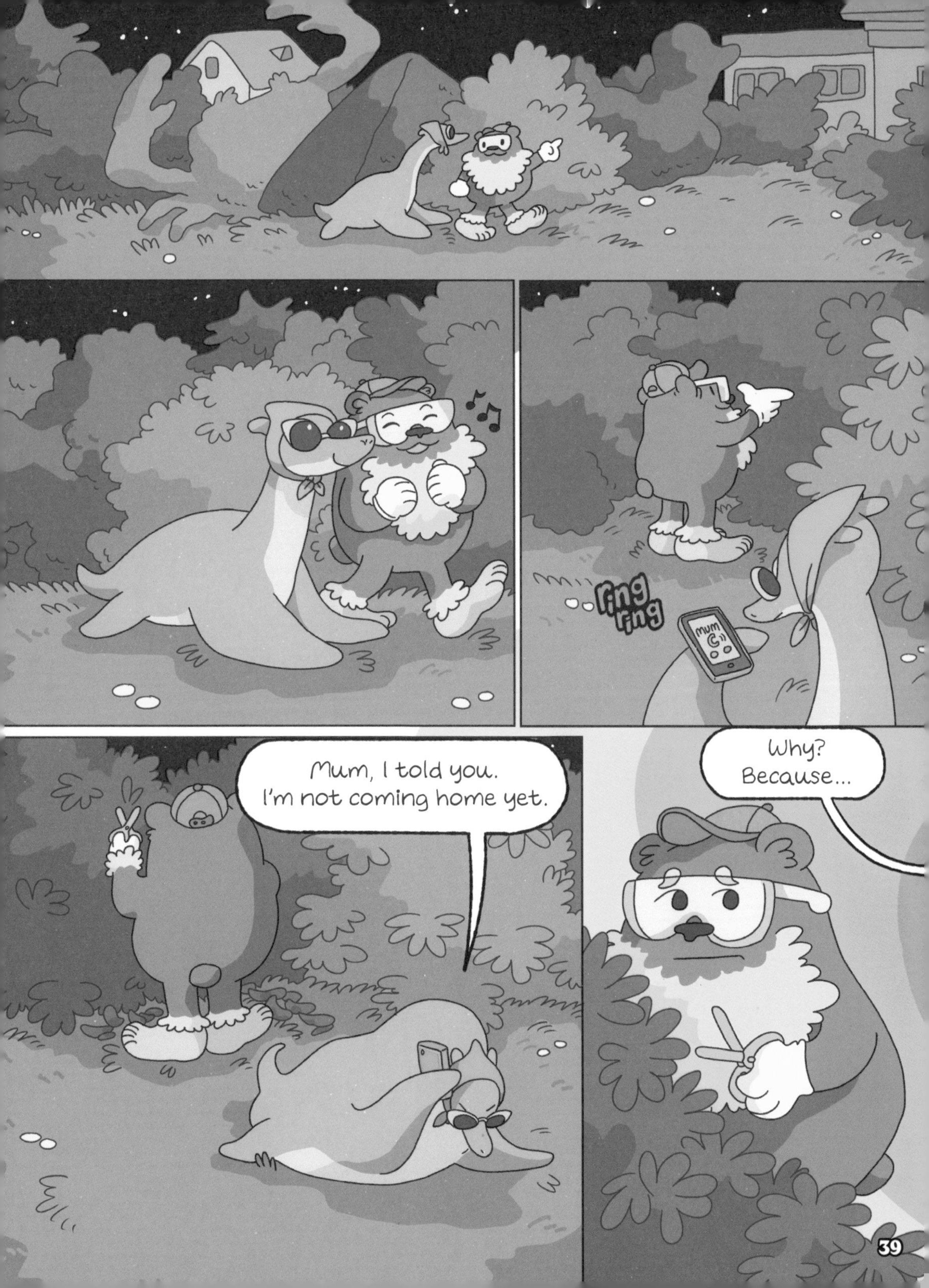
ring ring
mum
Mum, I told you.
I'm not coming home yet.
Why?
Because...

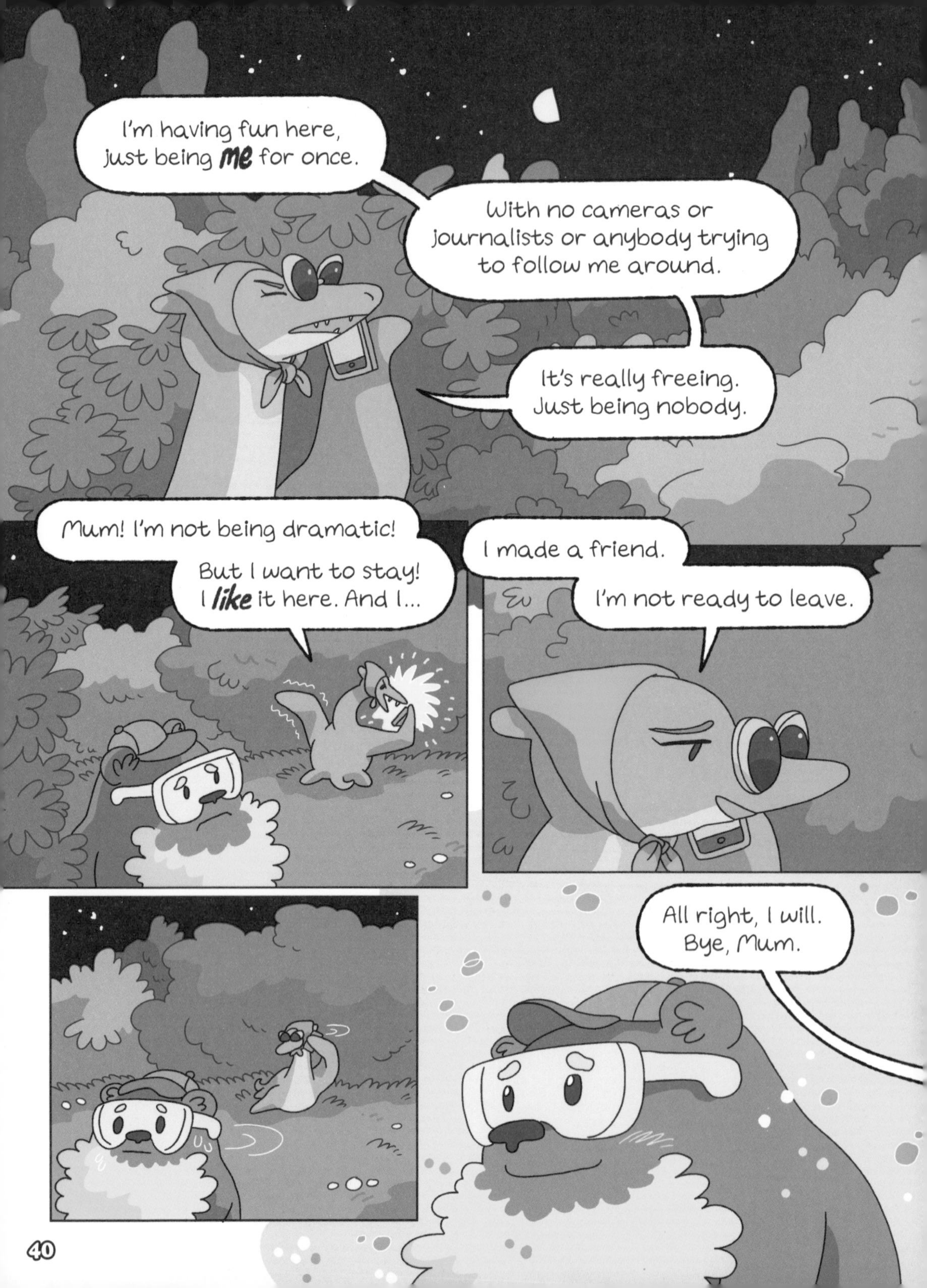
I'm having fun here, just being **ME** for once.
With no cameras or journalists or anybody trying to follow me around.
It's really freeing. Just being nobody.
Mum! I'm not being dramatic!
But I want to stay! I ***like*** it here. And I...
I made a friend.
I'm not ready to leave.
All right, I will. Bye, Mum.

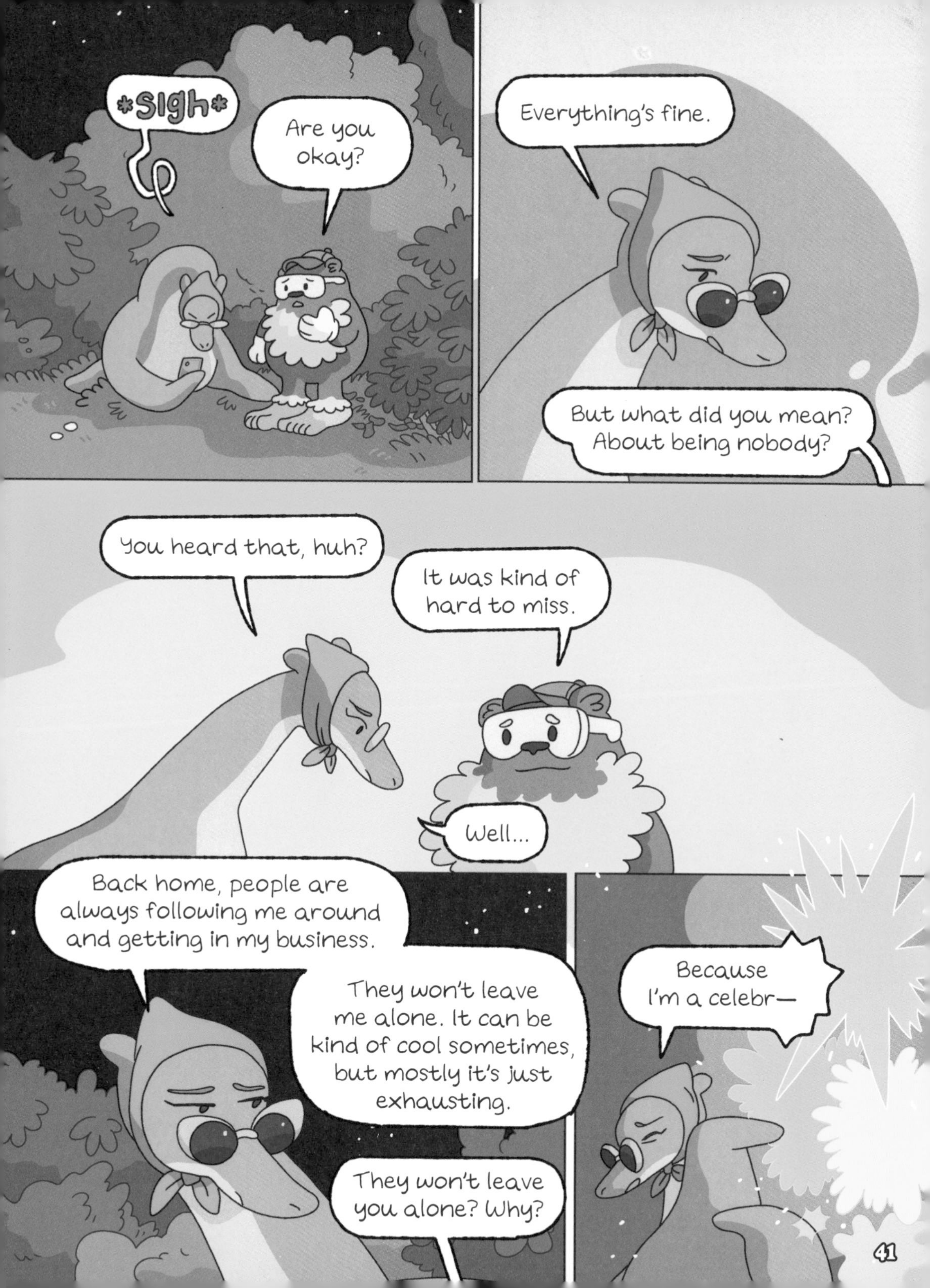
Sigh
Are you okay?
Everything's fine.
But what did you mean? About being nobody?
You heard that, huh?
It was kind of hard to miss.
Well...
Back home, people are always following me around and getting in my business.
They won't leave me alone. It can be kind of cool sometimes, but mostly it's just exhausting.
They won't leave you alone? Why?
Because I'm a celebr—

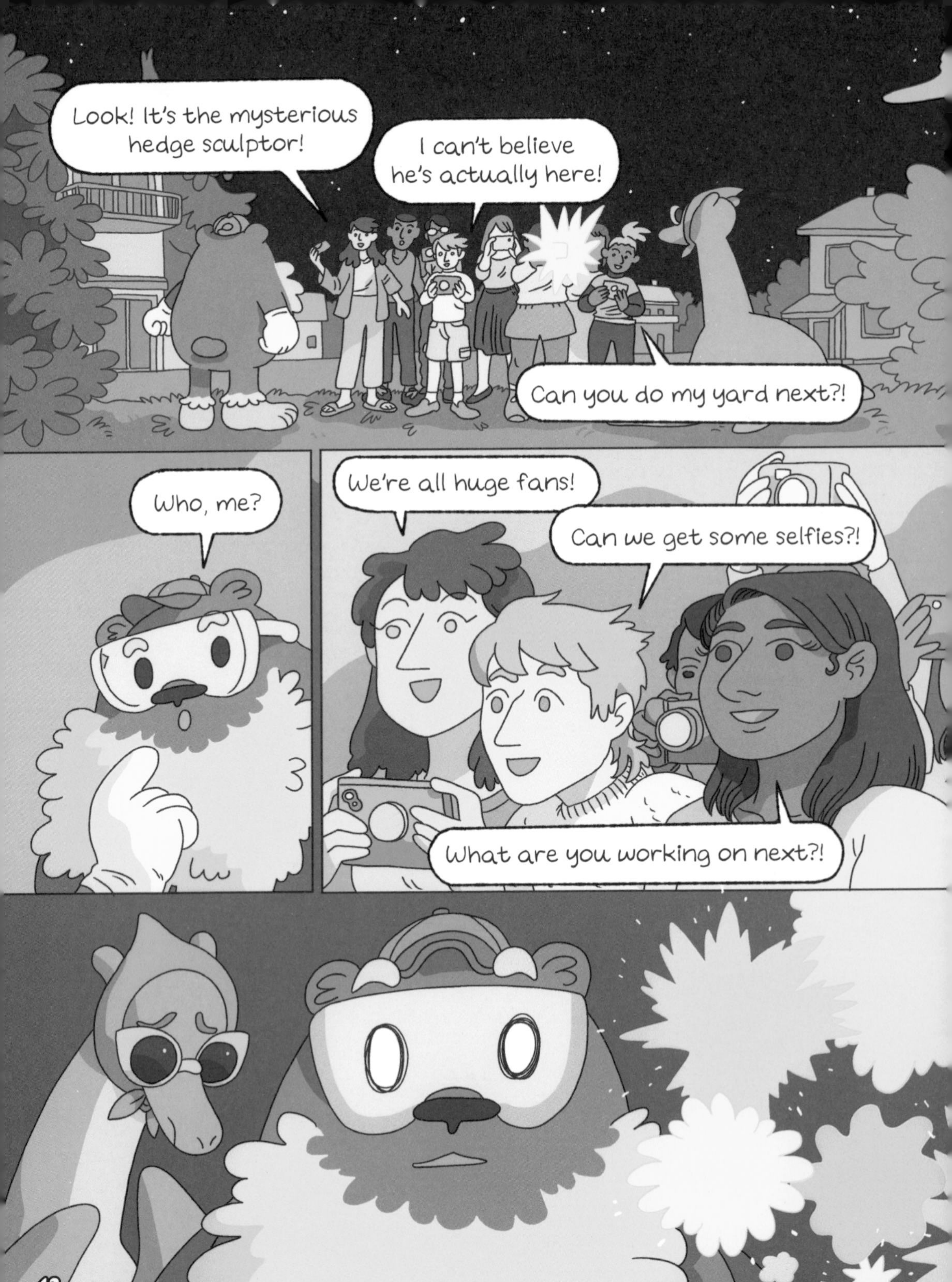
Look! It's the mysterious hedge sculptor!
I can't believe he's actually here!
Can you do my yard next?!
Who, me?
We're all huge fans!
Can we get some selfies?!
What are you working on next?!

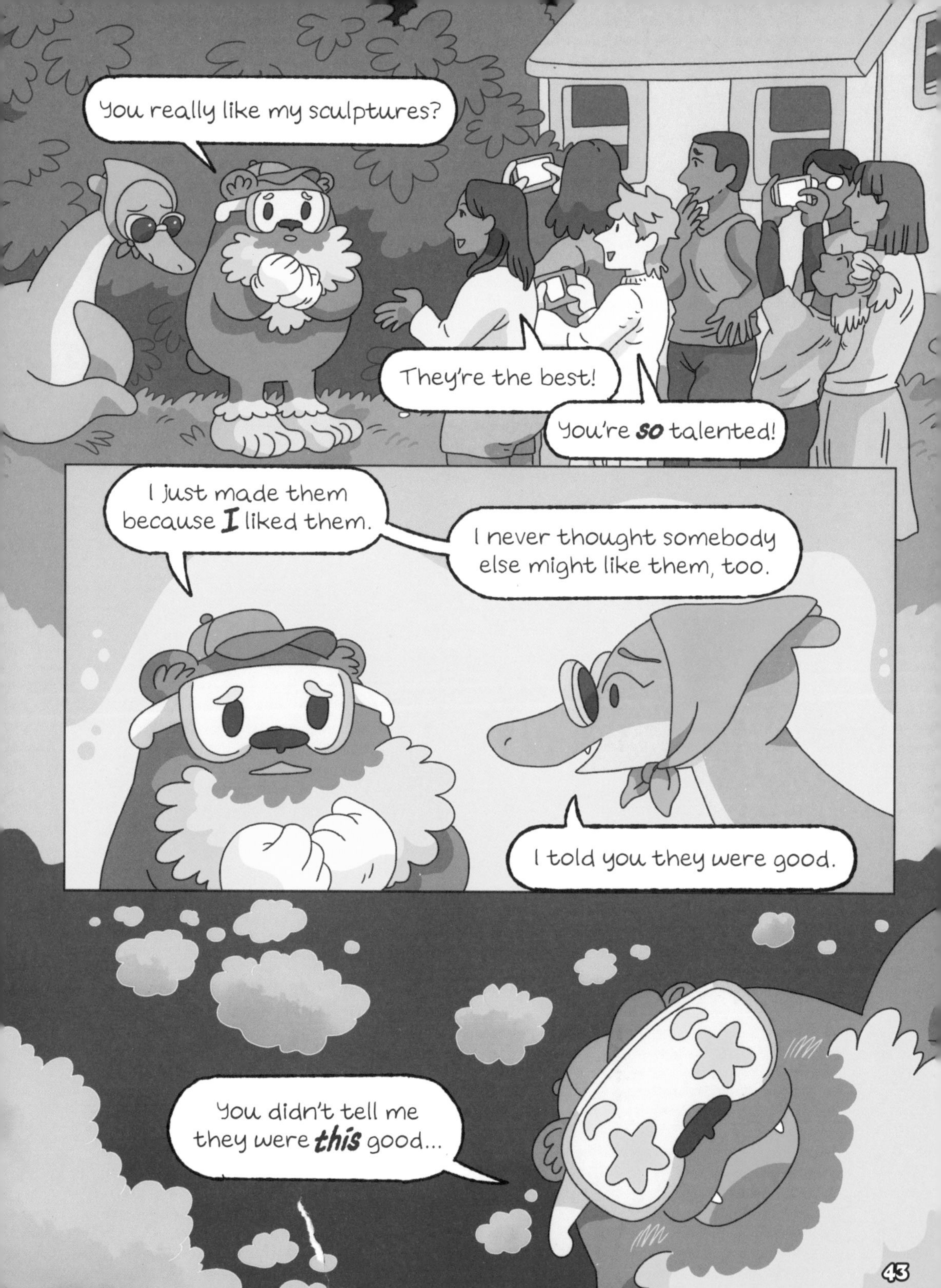
You really like my sculptures?
They're the best!
You're SO talented!
I just made them because I liked them.
I never thought somebody else might like them, too.
I told you they were good.
You didn't tell me they were this good...

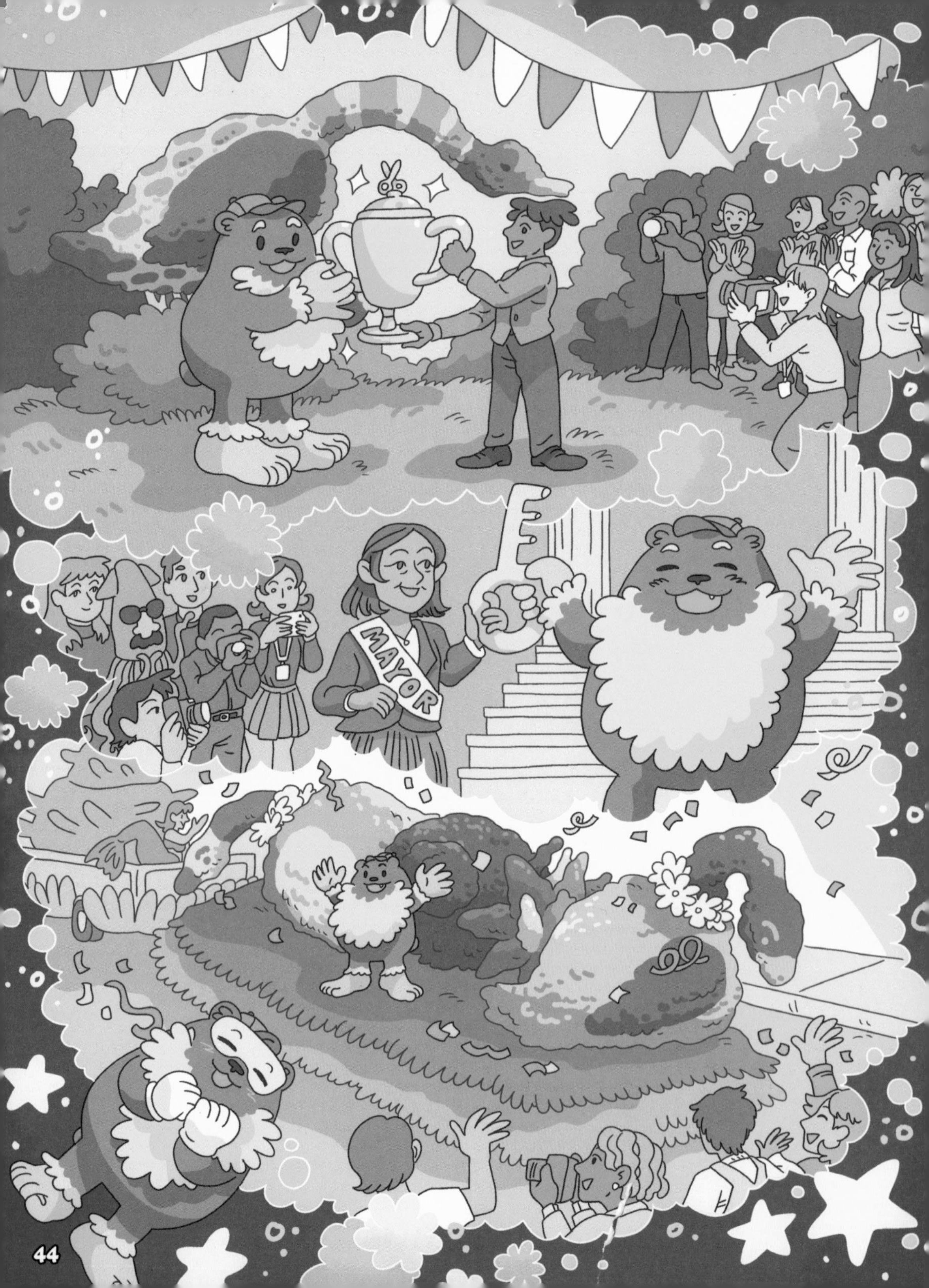
MAYOR

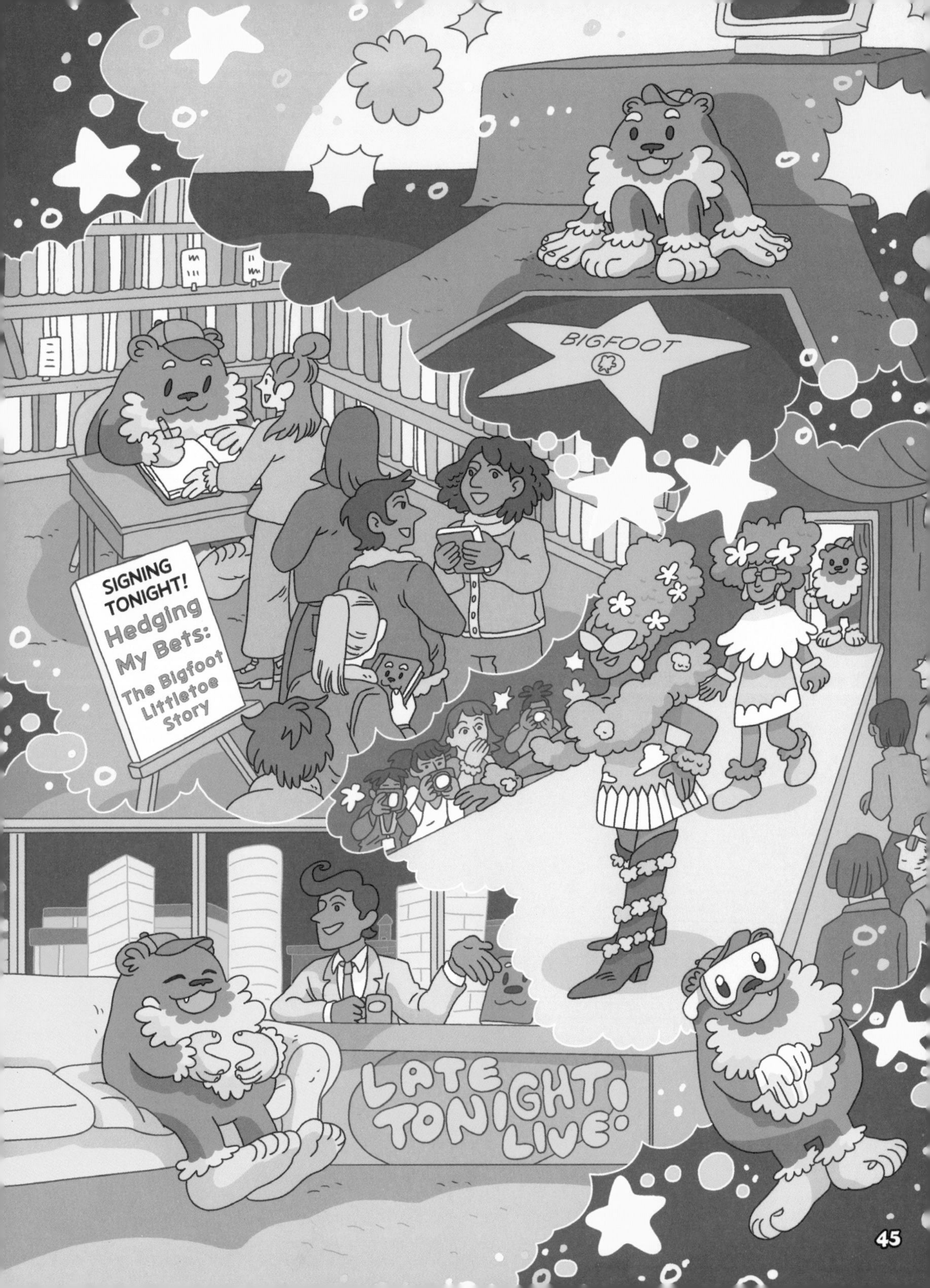
BIGFOOT
SIGNING TONIGHT!
Hedging My Bets:
The Bigfoot Littletoe Story
LATE TONIGHT LIVE!

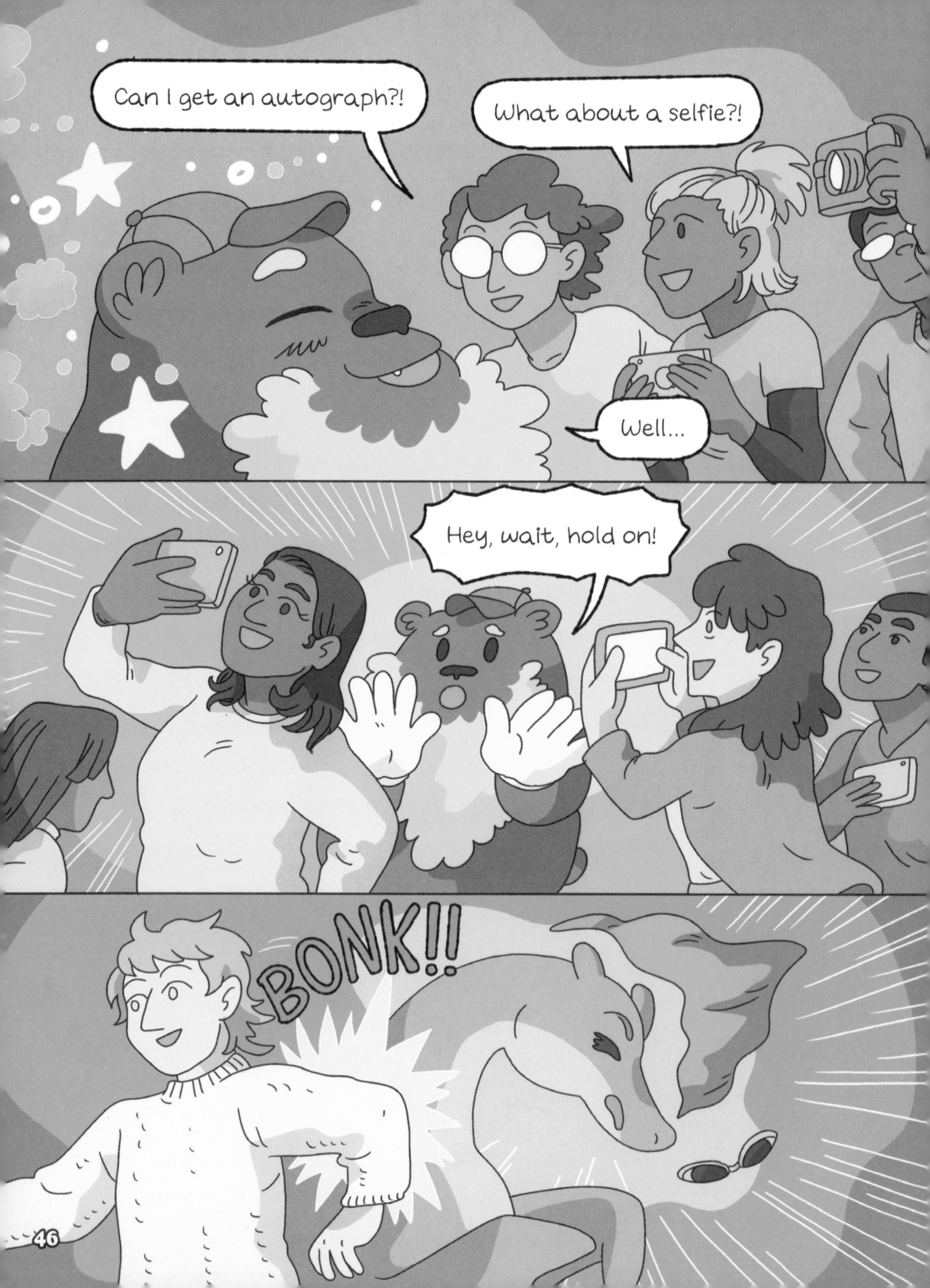

Can I get an autograph?!
What about a selfie?!
Well...
Hey, wait, hold on!
BONK!!

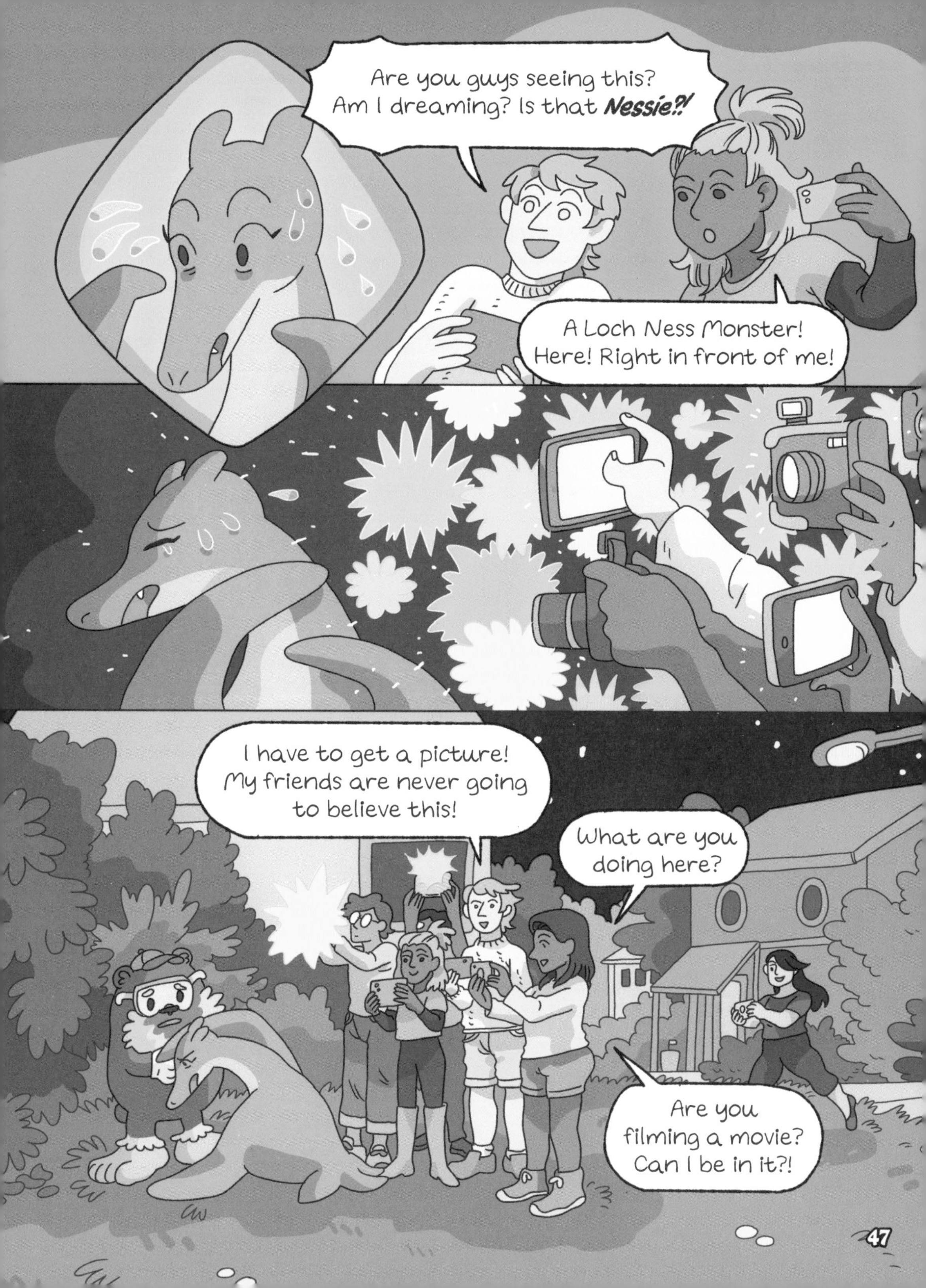
Are you guys seeing this? Am I dreaming? Is that **Nessie?!**
A Loch Ness Monster! Here! Right in front of me!
I have to get a picture! My friends are never going to believe this!
What are you doing here?
Are you filming a movie? Can I be in it?!

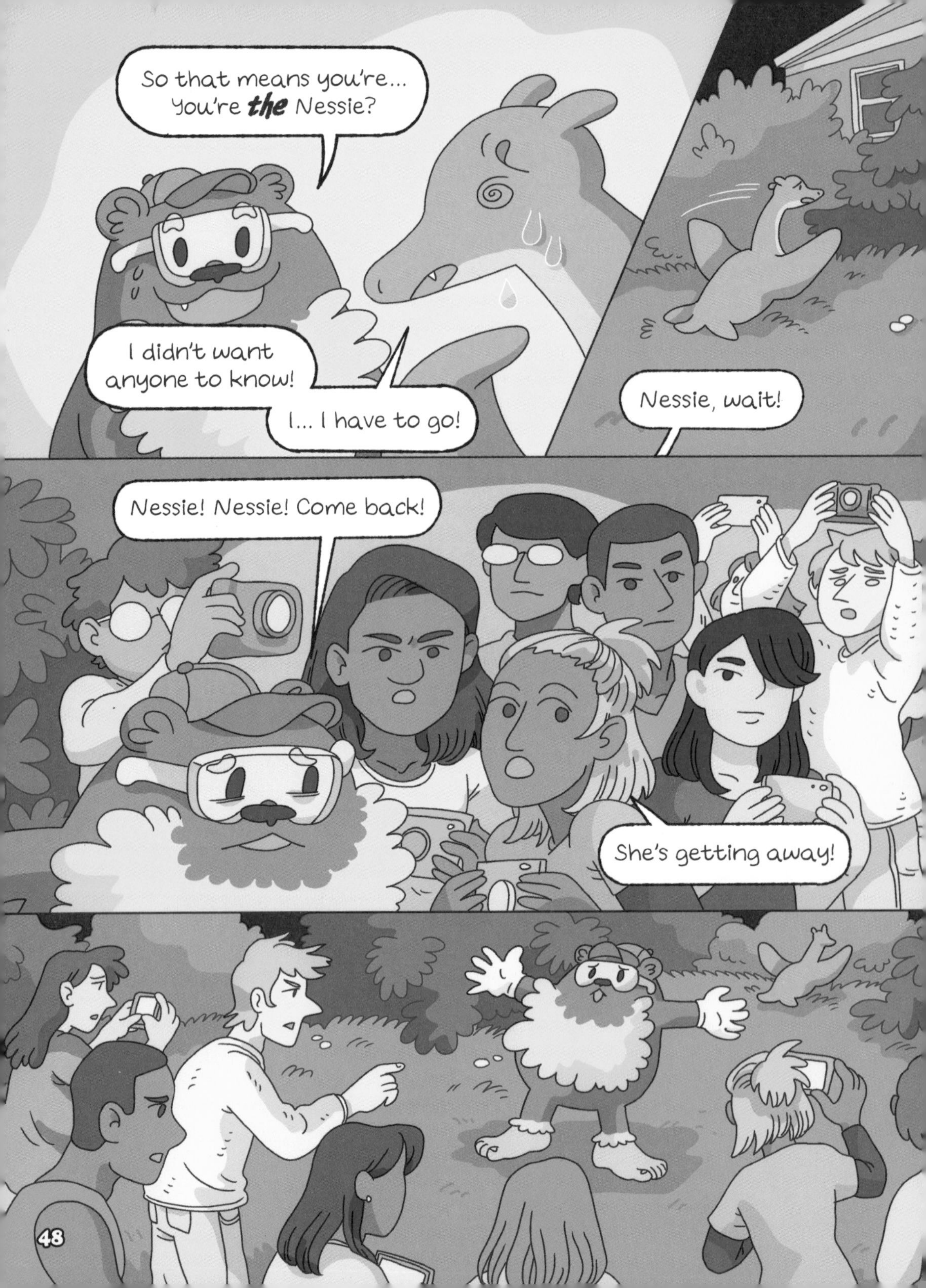
So that means you're... You're **the** Nessie?
I didn't want anyone to know!
I... I have to go!
Nessie, wait!
Nessie! Nessie! Come back!
She's getting away!

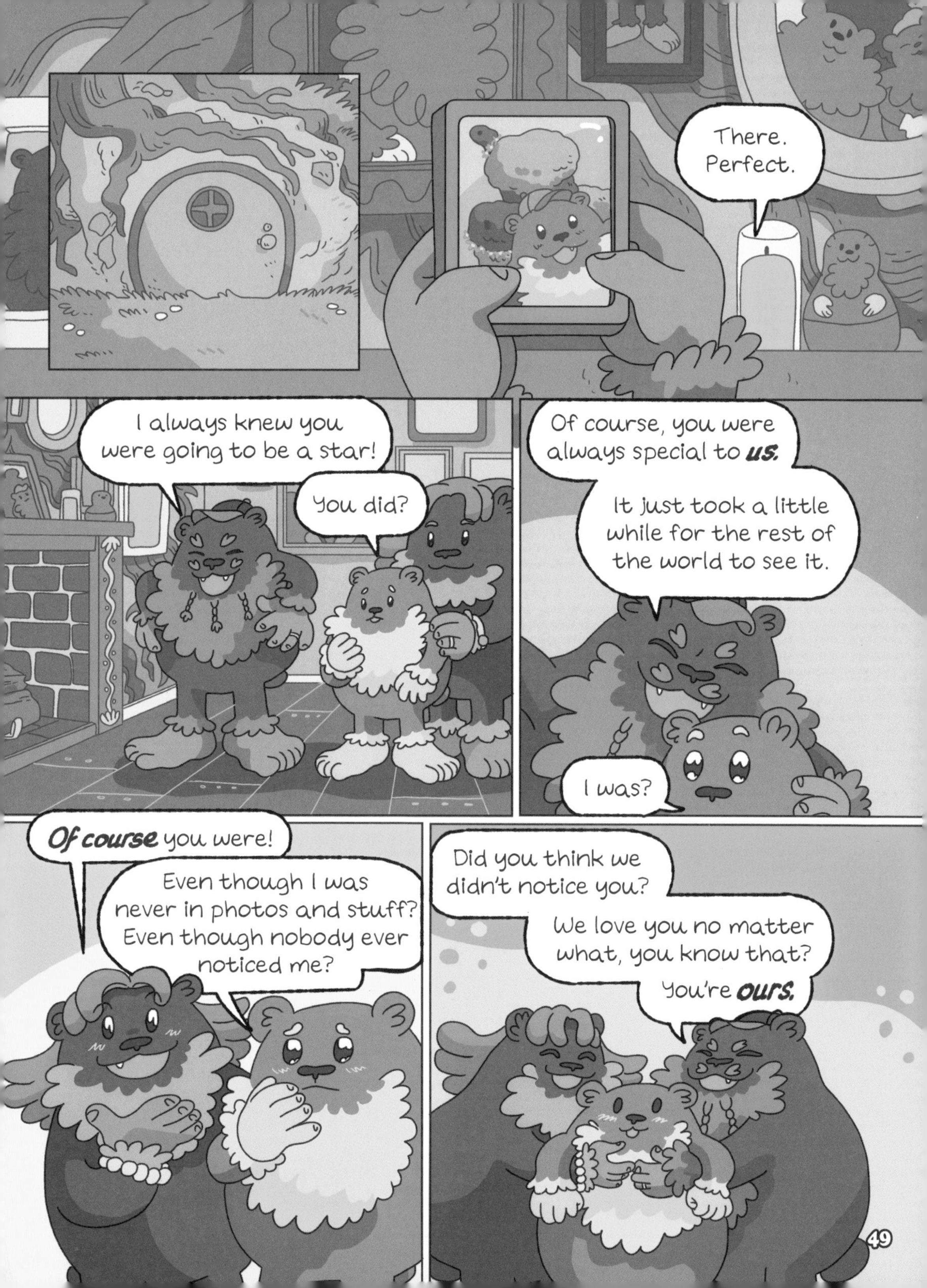
There. Perfect.
I always knew you were going to be a star!
You did?
Of course, you were always special to **us.**
It just took a little while for the rest of the world to see it.
I was?
Of course you were!
Even though I was never in photos and stuff? Even though nobody ever noticed me?
Did you think we didn't notice you?
We love you no matter what, you know that?
You're **ours.**

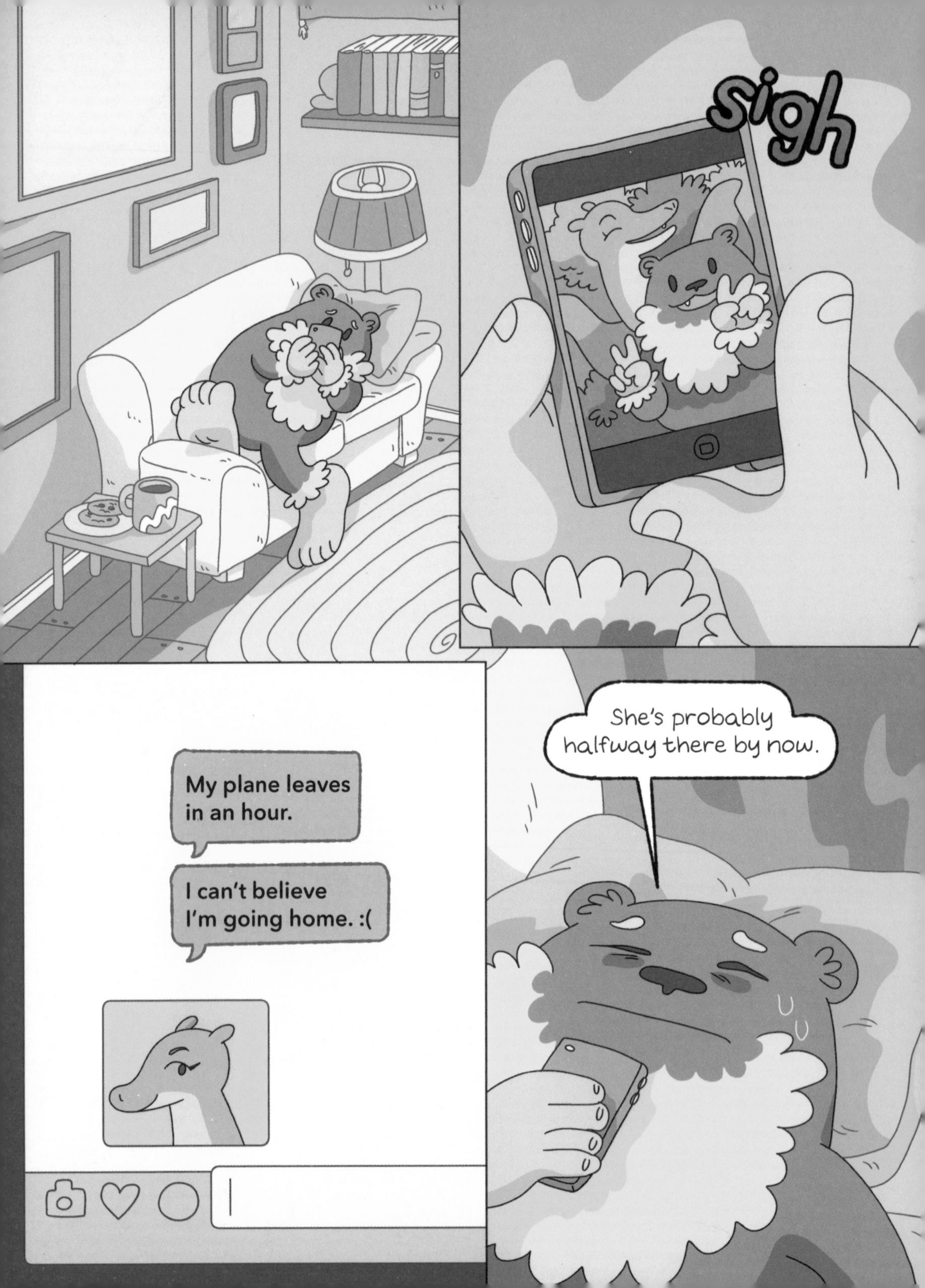
sigh
My plane leaves in an hour.
I can't believe I'm going home. :(
She's probably halfway there by now.

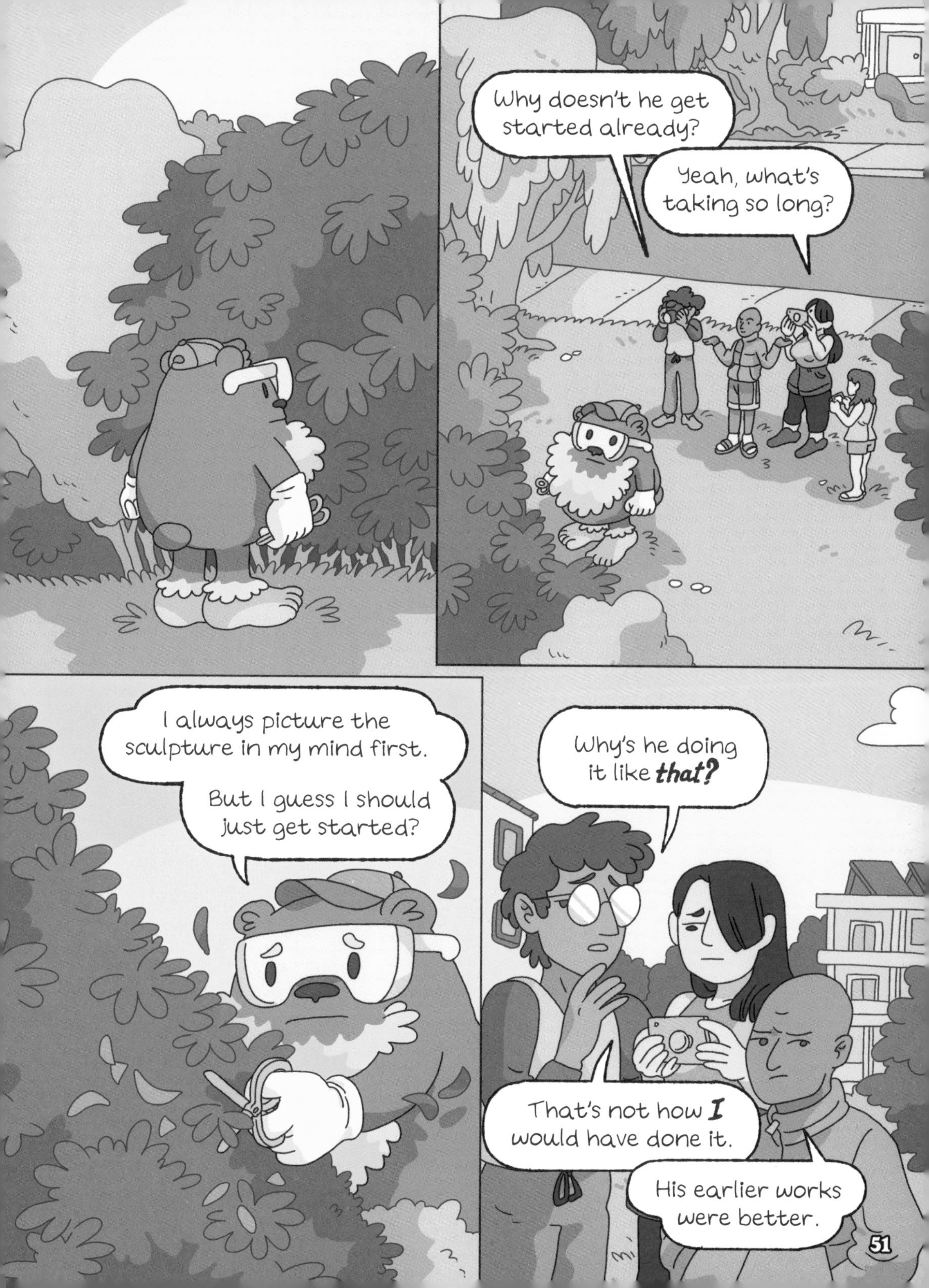
Why doesn't he get started already?
Yeah, what's taking so long?
I always picture the sculpture in my mind first.
But I guess I should just get started?
Why's he doing it like *that?*
That's not how *I* would have done it.
His earlier works were better.

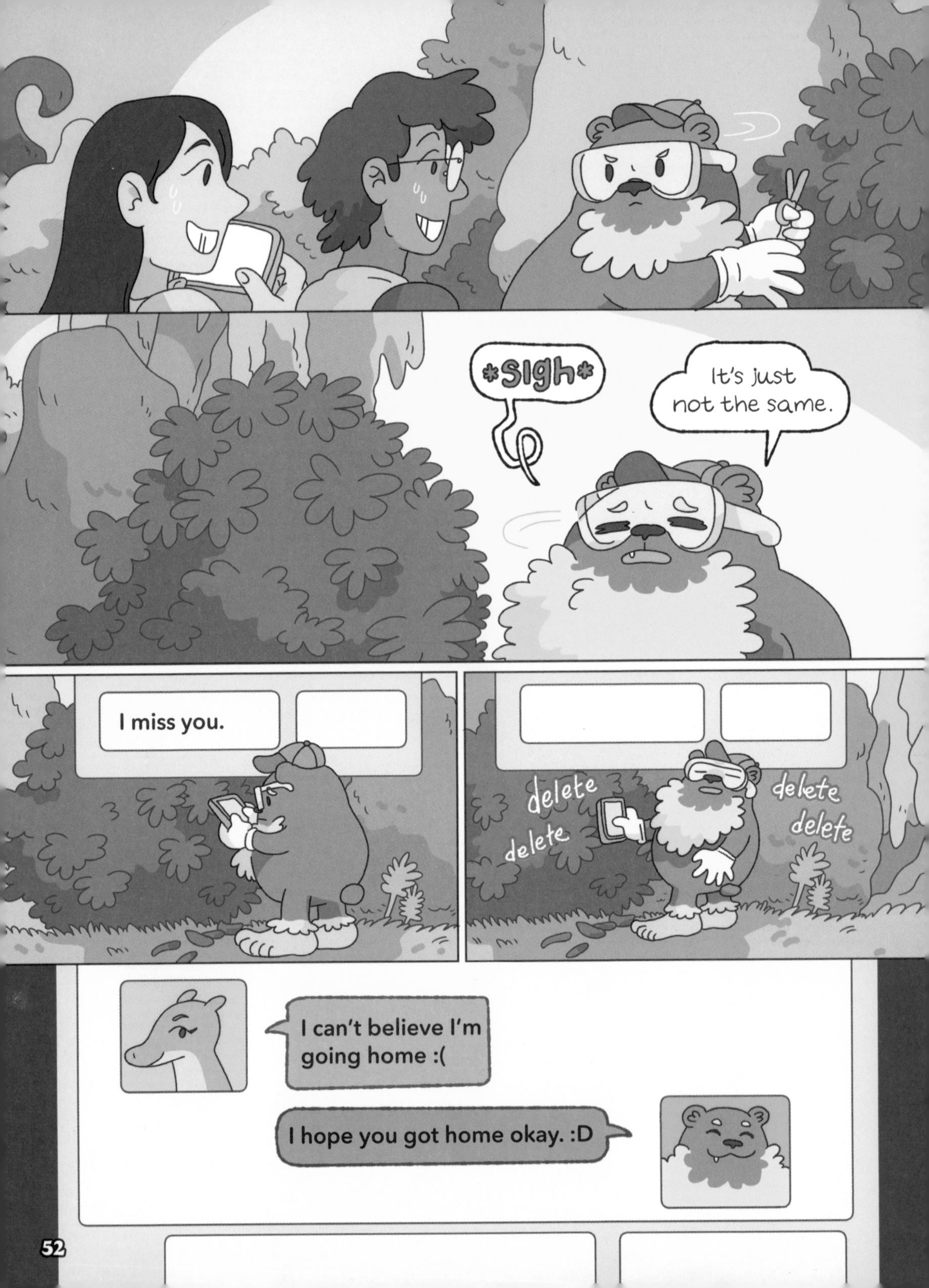
sigh
It's just not the same.
I miss you.
delete
delete
delete
delete
I can't believe I'm going home :(
I hope you got home okay. :D

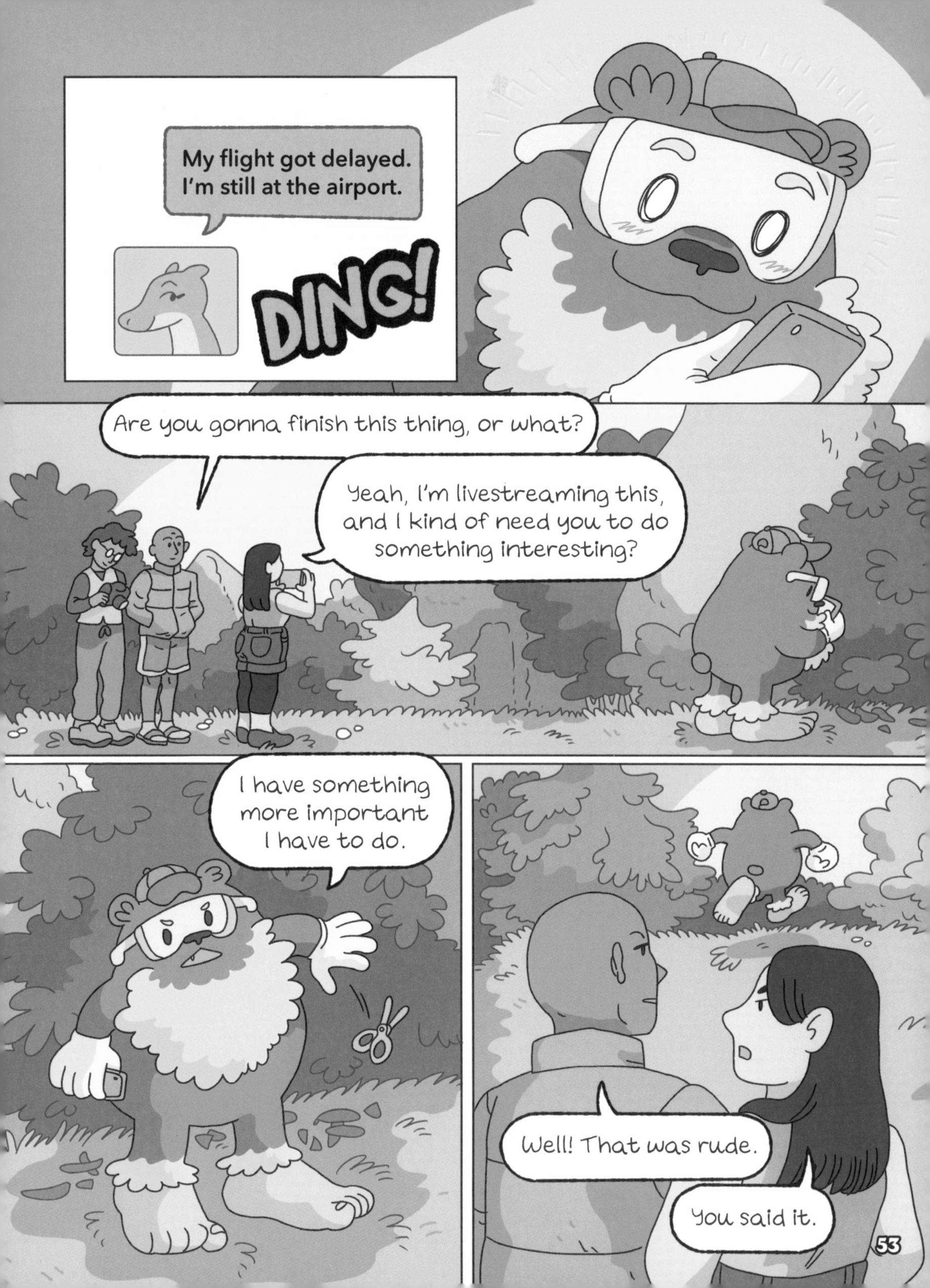
My flight got delayed. I'm still at the airport.
DING!
Are you gonna finish this thing, or what?
Yeah, I'm livestreaming this, and I kind of need you to do something interesting?
I have something more important I have to do.
Well! That was rude.
You said it.

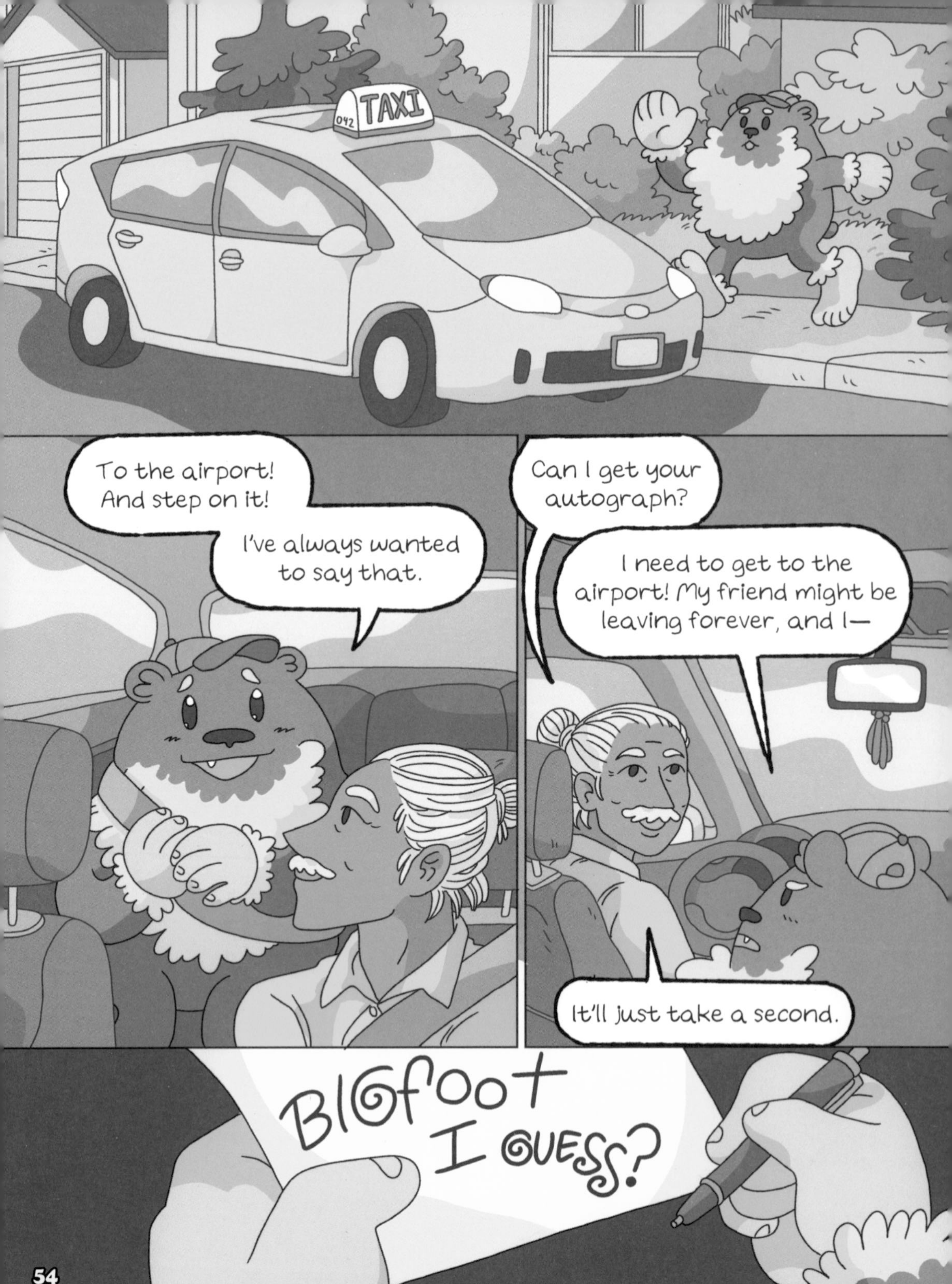
TAXI
042
To the airport! And step on it!
I've always wanted to say that.
Can I get your autograph?
I need to get to the airport! My friend might be leaving forever, and I—
It'll just take a second.
BIGfoot I GUESS?

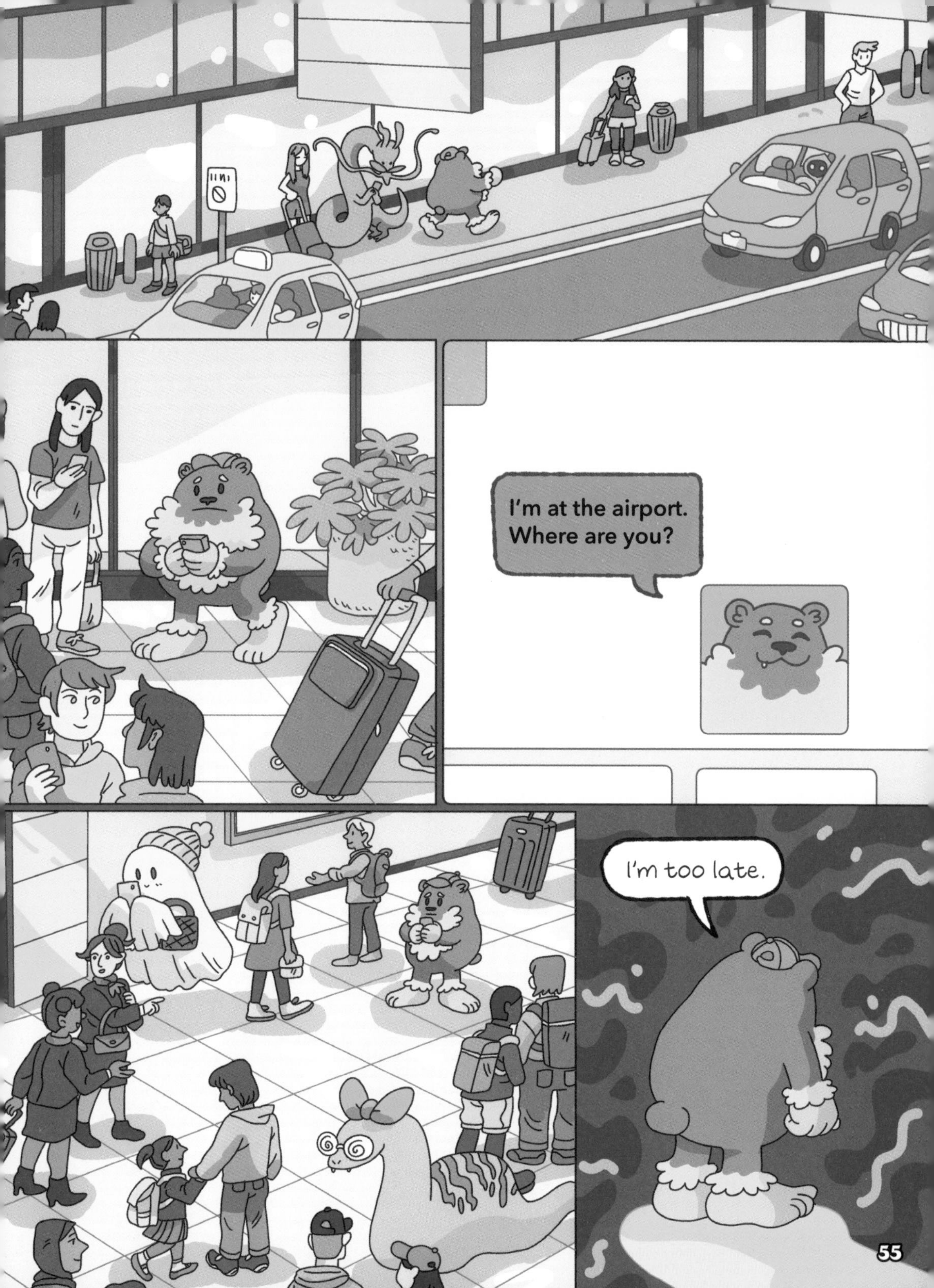
I'm at the airport.
Where are you?
I'm too late.

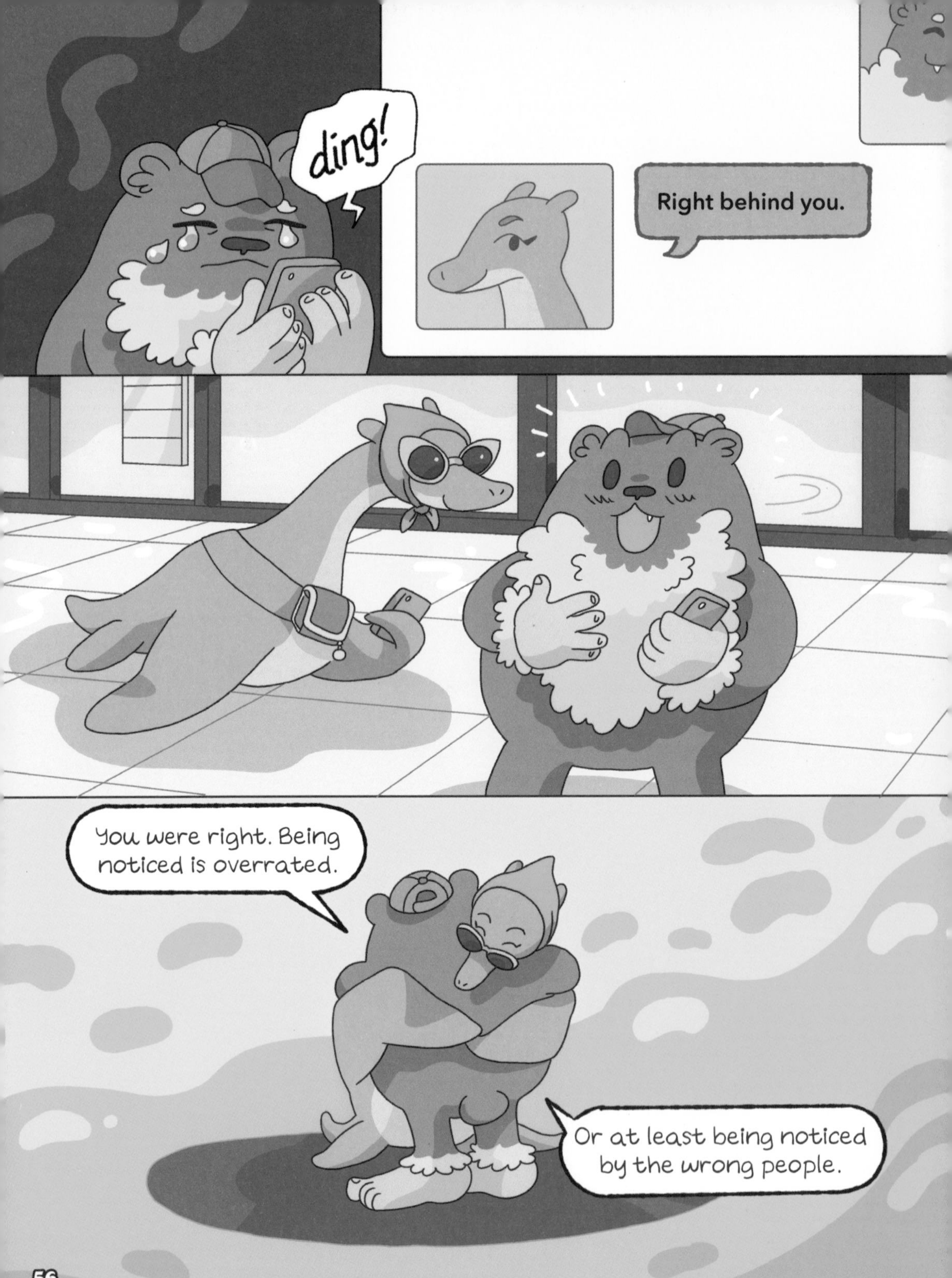
ding!
Right behind you.
You were right. Being noticed is overrated.
Or at least being noticed by the wrong people.

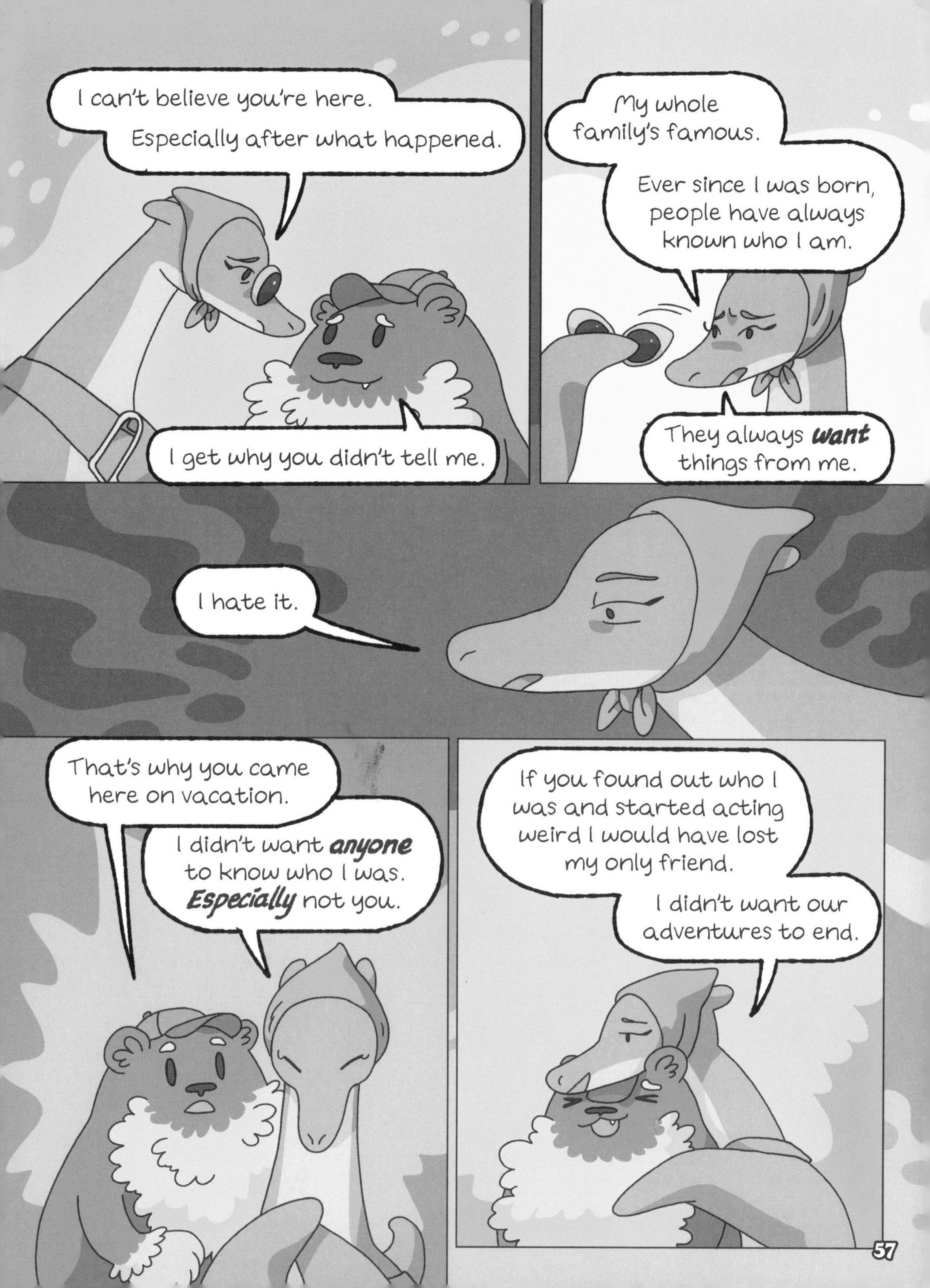
I can't believe you're here.
Especially after what happened.
I get why you didn't tell me.
My whole family's famous.
Ever since I was born, people have always known who I am.
They always **want** things from me.
I hate it.
That's why you came here on vacation.
I didn't want **anyone** to know who I was. **Especially** not you.
If you found out who I was and started acting weird I would have lost my only friend.
I didn't want our adventures to end.

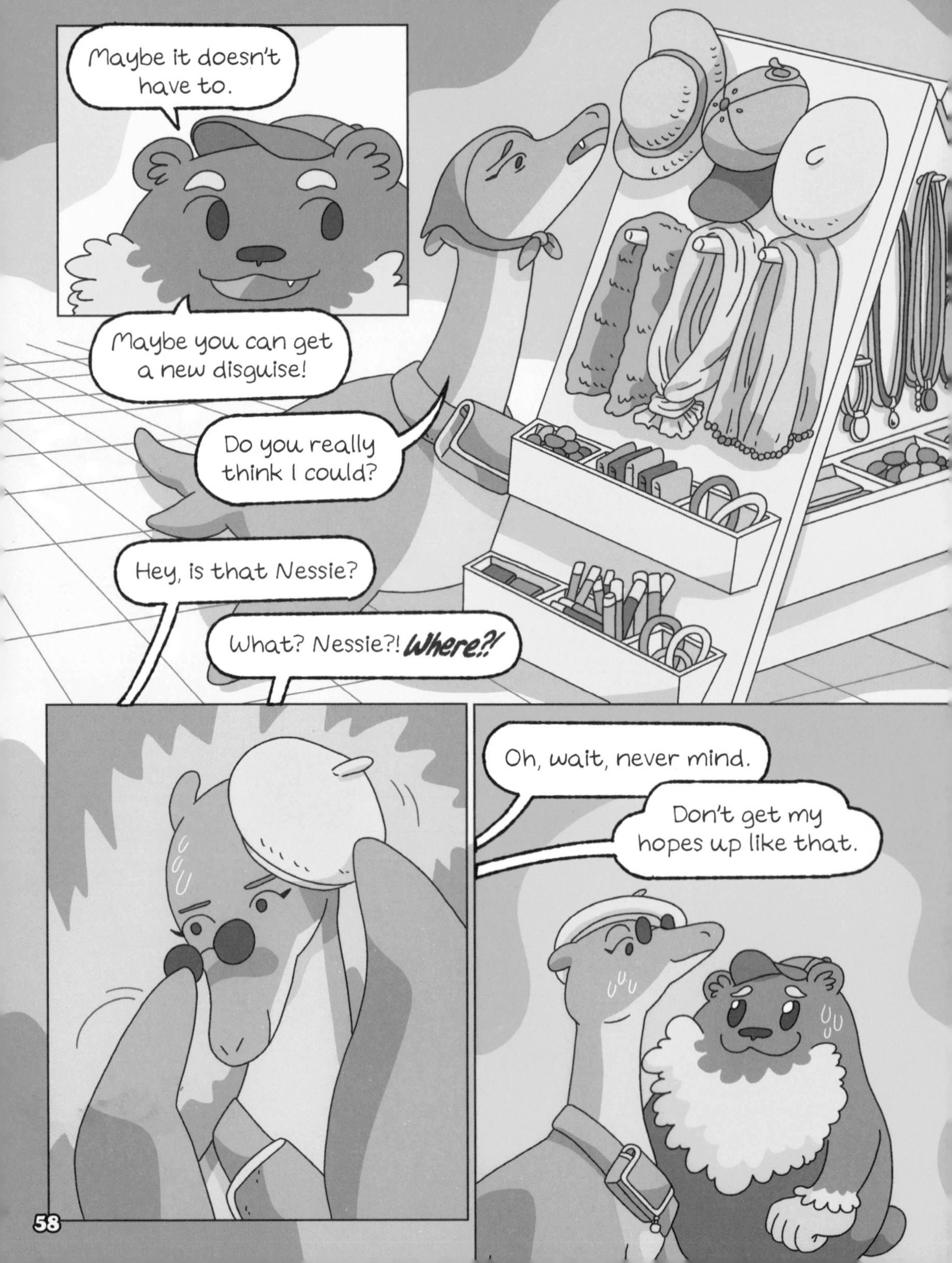
Maybe it doesn't have to.
Maybe you can get a new disguise!
Do you really think I could?
Hey, is that Nessie?
What? Nessie?! **Where?!**
Oh, wait, never mind.
Don't get my hopes up like that.

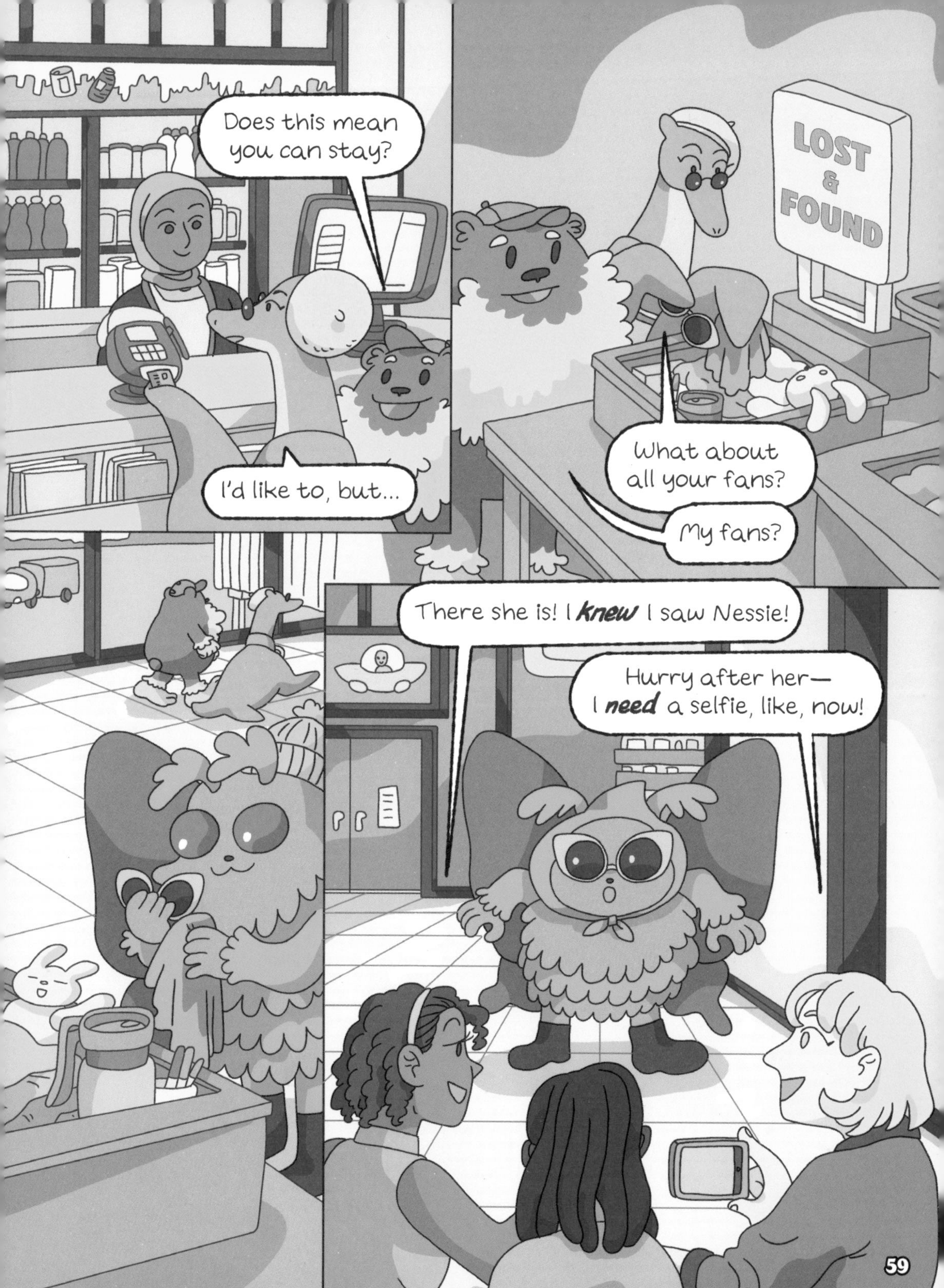
Does this mean you can stay?
I'd like to, but...
What about all your fans?
My fans?
LOST & FOUND
There she is! I *knew* I saw Nessie!
Hurry after her—I *need* a selfie, like, now!

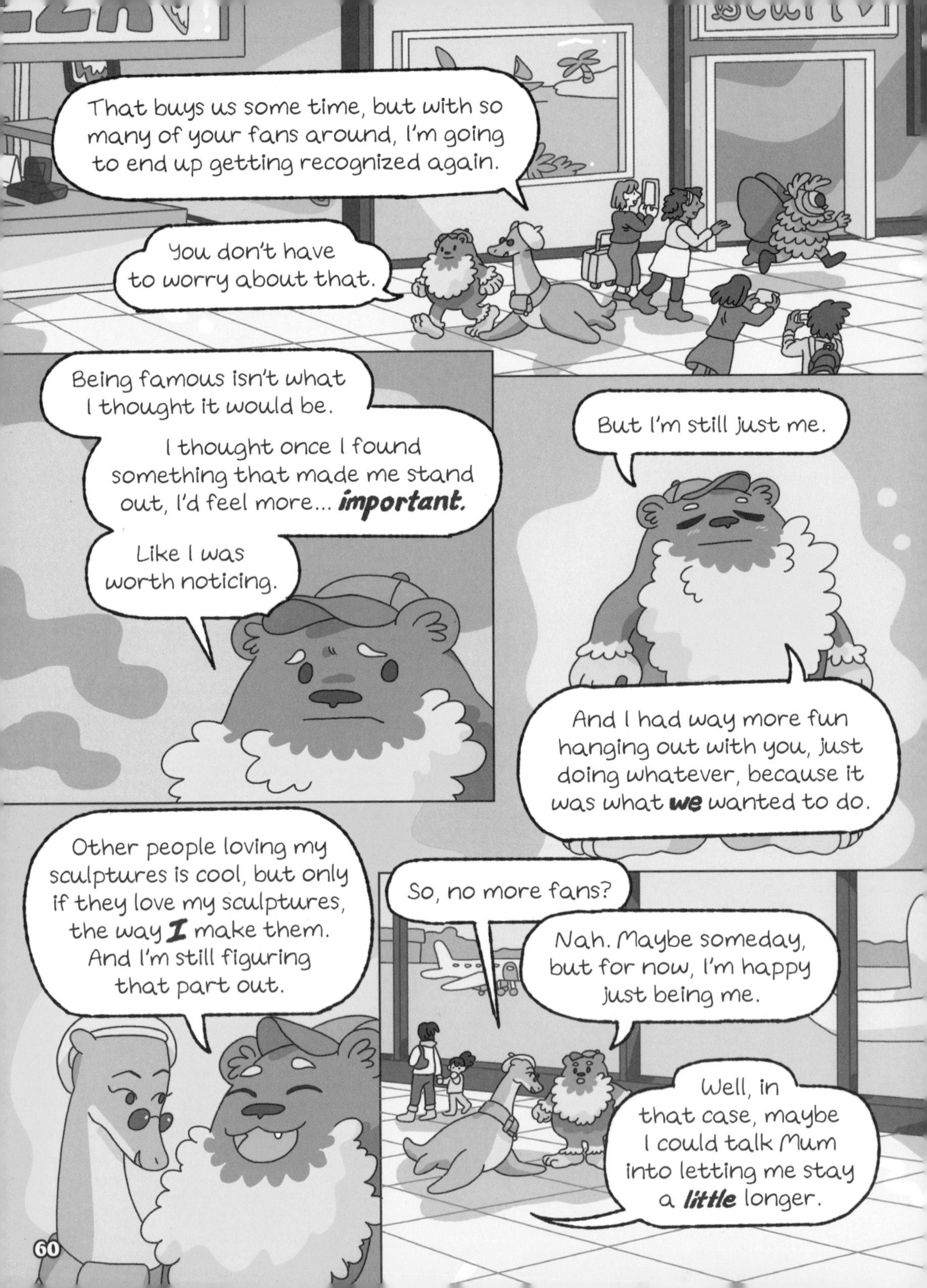
That buys us some time, but with so many of your fans around, I'm going to end up getting recognized again.
You don't have to worry about that.
Being famous isn't what I thought it would be.
I thought once I found something that made me stand out, I'd feel more... ***important.***
Like I was worth noticing.
But I'm still just me.
And I had way more fun hanging out with you, just doing whatever, because it was what ***we*** wanted to do.
Other people loving my sculptures is cool, but only if they love my sculptures, the way ***I*** make them. And I'm still figuring that part out.
So, no more fans?
Nah. Maybe someday, but for now, I'm happy just being me.
Well, in that case, maybe I could talk Mum into letting me stay a ***little*** longer.

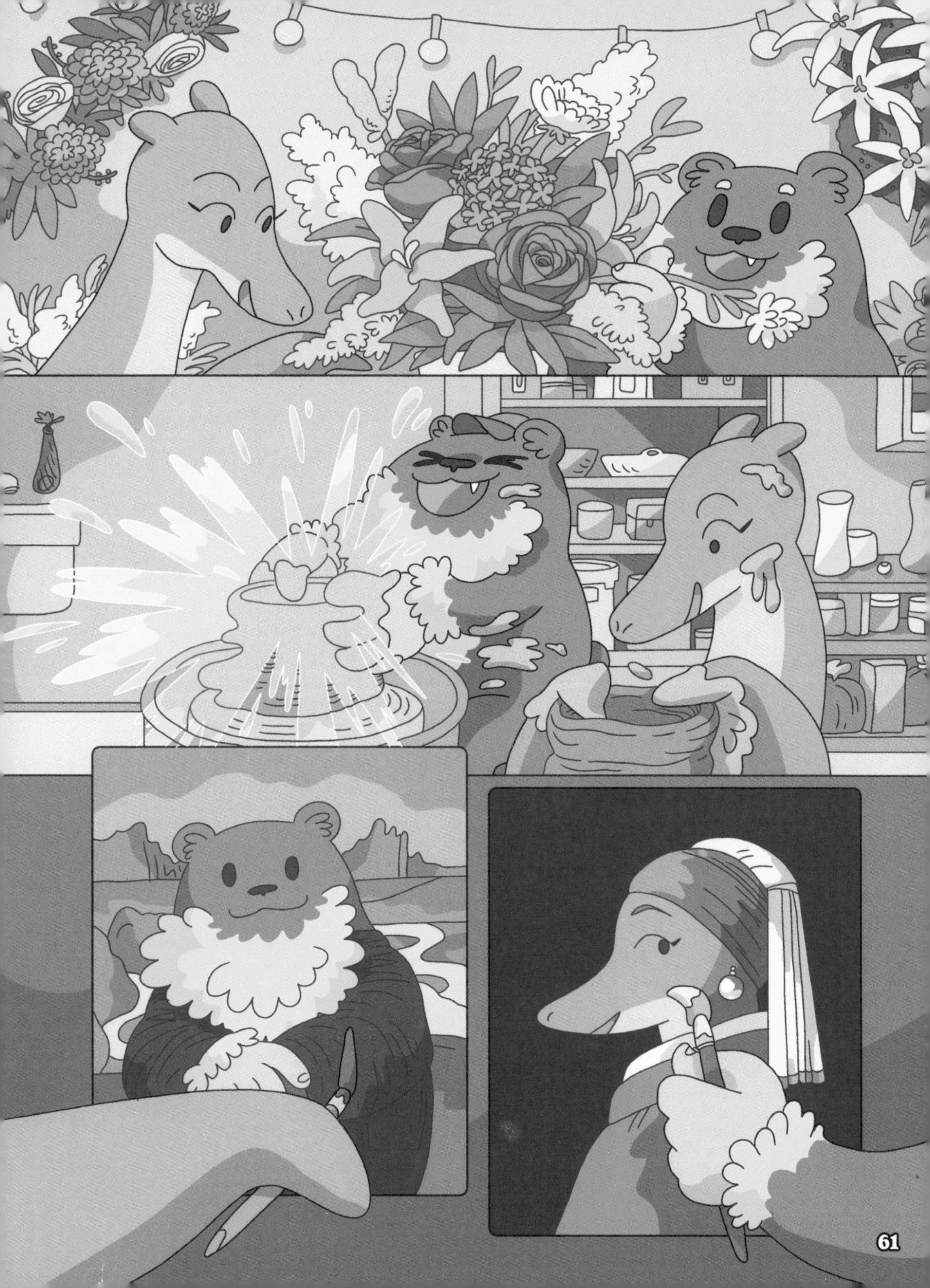

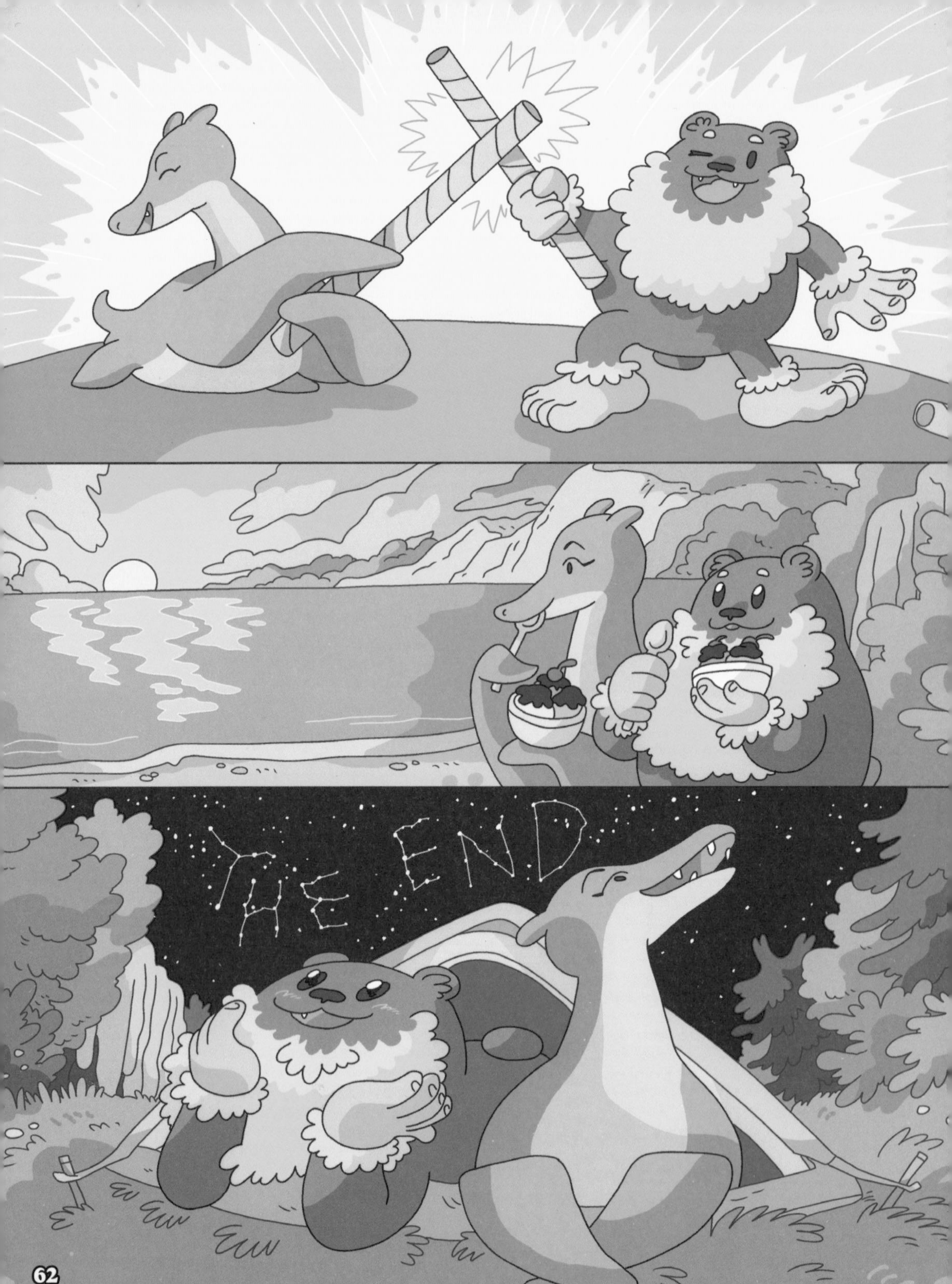
THE END

Chloe Tisdale

Chelsea M. Campbell

is always trying new things, which is why she wears a lot of hats. It's definitely not to disguise herself because she's secretly a cryptid. Besides writing this book, she's also the author of the Renegade X series for teens and creator of *The Weaver of Stories* video game. For more information—and to try and see what she looks like without a hat—you can visit her online at www.chelseamcampbell.com.

Priya Alahan

Laura Knetzger went to

the School of Visual Arts and graduated in 2012. Laura started drawing and self-publishing a series of all-ages comics called *Bug Boys* in 2011. Laura loves to make comics and books about small pleasures, small creatures, and feelings. The main inspirations for her stories come from plants and animals, art and handicrafts, and trying to think of things from a nonhuman perspective. She also enjoys painting, playing video games, and knitting. You can find her online at @LauraKnetzger.